MRS. TUESDAY'S DEPARTURE

Suzanne Elizabeth Anderson

Henry and George Press

Evergreen, Colorado

Mrs. Tuesday's Departure
By Suzanne Elizabeth Anderson

This is a work of fiction. Names, characters, places, and incidents are the product of the author's imagination or are used fictitiously, and any resemblance to actual persons, living or dead, business establishments, events, or locales is entirely coincidental.

Second Edition

ISBN-13: 978-1484870174
ISBN-10: 1484870174

Cover Design: GoOnWrite.com

For more information about the author and upcoming books, please visit: http://www.suzanneelizabethanderson.com

Published by
Henry and George Press
PO Box 2465
Evergreen, CO 80437

Please post a review on your favorite book site.

Your reviews have a tremendous impact on our success.

Thank you!

Books by Suzanne Elizabeth Anderson

Mrs. Tuesday's Departure

God Loves You. ~ Chester Blue

Trusting God with Your Dream

The Night of the Great Polar Bear

Love in a Time of War

A Map of Heaven

Henry's Guide to Happiness

God Loves Your Dream: A 60-Day Devotional Journey Toward God's Dream for You

Dios Te Ama –Chester Blue

Confiandole Nuestros Suenos a Dios

For my mother

Adeline Lucas Anderson

Her love and encouragement
makes everything possible.

Now faith is the substance of things hoped for, the evidence of things not seen.
~ Hebrews 11:1 King James Version

Prologue

Once upon a time, in a future far away, seventy years after the end of the War …

The old woman dropped the unopened package onto the edge of the sofa. Pausing for a moment, she took in the room: the magnificent mahogany armoire and card table, the tall windows whose rich brocade curtains always stood open so that she could appreciate what little light came into the room. She was glad that soon she would leave it behind forever.

At the front door, she put on her coat and wound a red cashmere scarf around her neck. She closed the door behind her, locked it, and then waited patiently for the elevator as she tugged on her black leather gloves.

"Good evening, Mrs. Tuesday," the elevator

operator said as the steel doors rolled closed in front of them. "How are you this evening?" He thought she looked a bit pale, thinner through the cheeks.

"I'm well, Patrick," Mrs. Tuesday said as she watched the numbers descend.

"Watch your step, Ma'am," said Patrick as she stepped out and into the lobby.

The gilt mirrors on opposite walls were still trimmed with Christmas garland and adorned with red velvet bows that matched the camelback sofas beneath.

Her heels clicked and echoed as she crossed the lobby's black and white marble tiles. She rarely saw any of her neighbors, though the building was large, with two or three apartments on each floor. "Quietly elegant" was how she'd heard a realtor describe the property. "Old money," she heard the realtor whisper when she thought Mrs. Tuesday was out of range. Mrs. Tuesday chuckled. The money belonged to her late husband, and the only thing old about it was her age.

"Good evening," she said to the doorman who held open the front door.

"Good evening, Mrs. Tuesday, on your way to Mass?"

mrs. tuesday's departure

She smiled and nodded at the young man dressed in the same maroon wool uniform that all the building staff wore. He was new, and she peered at his nametag. She tugged a red felt beret halfway down her forehead and over the tops of her ears. "Thank you, Joseph."

"Let me get you a taxi," he said, taking her elbow as she stepped out onto the icy sidewalk. "You shouldn't walk in this weather."

Mrs. Tuesday shook her head. "The church is only four blocks away, and I'll be fine."

"You wait right here," Joseph said, already turning back toward the door. "I'll grab my coat and walk you there."

"You'll get in trouble."

Joseph laughed, "I won't. I've made a sign just for these occasions."

They linked arms and began a slow walk up Park Avenue toward St. Catherine's, the little Catholic Church where Mrs. Tuesday attended the evening mass, daily, for the last fifty years, of her married, and now widowed life in New York. They bowed their heads against the cold and followed the fresh tracks in the snow-covered sidewalk. When she peered out there was little to see, the apartment buildings formed an ochre-brown canyon of hunch-backed beasts with light-speckled hides. The falling snow dimmed the streetlights and cast a gloomy steel shadow.

Little had changed in this part of the city. The shops that occupied space at street level reflected the style and wealth of the times. The grocer on the corner had changed its name three times over the years, but remained a place to buy eggs. The most disturbing change was the atmosphere.

There was something uncomfortably metallic; an electric hum replaced the hum of air conditioners that years ago adorned every window in the city. There were more people now, there were always more. Though the storm had thinned vehicular and pedestrian traffic, quieting the neighborhood, Mrs. Tuesday still perceived the annoying grating the layers of snow muffled, but could not hide.

As her heel slipped on a patch of ice, Joseph's hand tightened around her arm. "It's a good thing I came along," he said.

She agreed, reluctantly. Mrs. Tuesday treasured her independence, hated the aches and pains and need for help from others that had come gradually and then swiftly after she'd turned eighty. "Do you have plans for the New Year's Eve?" she asked.

"I'm taking my girlfriend down to Times Square. She wants to see the ball drop. I told her she was crazy, but this is her first year in the city."

A rapid staccato that sounded like gunshots followed by a thunderous boom reverberated swiftly through the apartment-lined canyon. Joseph's gentle hand tightened around her arm. "They're starting the fireworks early this year."

Fireworks didn't scare her. Rather, it was the memory of bombs, the flames that consumed the buildings and their inhabitants. It was the scream of the rockets that sounded so much like the last shrill warning of the trains that filled the station before their departure, taking all she loved.

Mrs. Tuesday remembered the raw excitement of the city in the early years after her arrival. She'd been twelve then, spoke little English, an orphan of the war sent to live with strangers. She'd always imagined her exile would be temporary that one day her mother would rescue her, and they would return to Hungary together.

Eventually, she realized being assigned the role of mother did not ensure reliability or the reciprocation of love. The years passed, and she grew up and discarded childish dreams. Instead, she took a job, got married, had a child, and then became old.

"My husband and I watched the ball drop for the Millennium. We weren't actually down on the street, we watched from a friend's apartment. But that was fifteen years ago."

"Fifteen years, I was just a kid," Joseph laughed.

Mrs. Tuesday paused in front of the church doors. "Thank you for walking me here."

"I'll come back and pick you up after Mass, how long do you need?"

Mrs. Tuesday sighed knowing she had no choice in the matter and secretly grateful for his insistence, "About an hour, I appreciate your kindness."

She'd stopped in the middle of the sidewalk in front of the church. She stared up at the heavy wooden doors and the darkened entrance that emitted only the faintest twinkling of candlelight. Perhaps she should go back for the package.

mrs. tuesday's departure

Inside, the church was nearly as dark as the evening outside. There were few people in attendance, perhaps five, old women like herself, coats on against the cold, backs bent under osteoporosis, little silver heads craning upwards toward the crucifix like turtles craning from their shells.

Mrs. Tuesday walked up the aisle to the fourth pew on the right, nodding as she passed familiar faces. She made a shallow genuflection, crossed herself, and scuttled sideways into the pew. Her arthritic knees no longer permitted her to kneel, so she perched on the edge of the wooden bench, and held her rosary in her hands as she said her prayers.

Even after all these years, gazing at the image of Christ on the Cross could still move her to tears. Yes, she knew He was no longer there, had died, was buried, and then rose again on the third day.

It was a familiar line she recited at every Mass. But the miracle of the Resurrection wasn't the source of her awe; it was the love Jesus shared in his willingness to go to the cross in the first place.

She watched Father Menendez hobble to the altar,

and she slid back on the pew and tucked her rosary into her pocket. The depth of that love brought her to Christ as a young girl and kept her enthralled for the rest of her life.

"In the name of the Father, the Son, and the Holy Spirit," Father Menendez said as he crossed himself. He was nearly as old as she was, but there were too few priests these days to allow an able-bodied man, like Father Menendez, to retire.

"Amen," answered Mrs. Tuesday and the rest of the old women.

When Mass was completed, Mrs. Tuesday walked over to the statue of the Virgin Mary and gazed into the eyes of the benevolent Mother. She stuffed a dollar into the box and then lighted two candles as she did every day. "For those who sacrificed so we could live," she whispered.

She thought of the unopened package at home, the phone calls that had preceded it the plane reservations she'd made, hoping to hurry its arrival. After all these years of wondering, the answers were in that envelope, yet she had not had the courage to open it.

She hesitated and then reached into her purse and

stuffed another dollar into the coin box. Her hand shook as she guided the wooden skewer with another flame to a new candle. "For my daughter."

~*~

At home, Mrs. Tuesday took off her coat, put on her slippers, warmed a cup of consommé, and settled into a chair in the living room. She placed the package on the table next to two leather journals and a stack of typed pages. She checked her watch and waited.

The grandfather clock chimed eight o'clock, there was a knock on the door, and a key turned in the lock. Mrs. Tuesday watched the door open and smiled as her granddaughter came in.

"I'm sorry I'm late," she said as she bent over to kiss Mrs. Tuesday. "I was at the library."

"There's coffee in the kitchen, pour a cup and come sit with me."

Mrs. Tuesday watched her granddaughter come back into the living room. She was tall; her brunette hair fell halfway down her back and over her shoulders.

She looked like the typical college student, jeans,

turtleneck, boots, and eyes tired from late nights of studying but glittering with the optimism of youth. She sat cross-legged on the couch and sipped her coffee.

"Are you well Grandma?"

"I'm fine, maybe a little touch of the flu," Mrs. Tuesday touched her chest. "How are your studies?"

Her granddaughter rolled her eyes. "I don't know why a writer has to take biology and calculus."

Mrs. Tuesday chuckled, "They will make you a better writer. How is your novel coming?"

"I made the changes you suggested last time, and I've brought you three more chapters to read."

Mrs. Tuesday lifted her reading glasses to the bridge of her nose and took the pages from her granddaughter's hands. She had moved back into the city to attend college. After her parents divorced, her granddaughter and her mother moved to Long Island and Mrs. Tuesday watched Mila grow up on weekend visits and holidays. With each visit, Mrs. Tuesday had brought books for her granddaughter to read. Her granddaughter's maturation measured by her progression from the fairy tales of Hans Christen Andersen, to Little Women, Jane Eyre and then novels that her granddaughter checked out from the library.

Her granddaughter had expressed an early interest in writing. At the age of eleven, she had begun sending Mrs. Tuesday short stories to 'edit'. When she was old enough to come into the city alone, they had begun these monthly meetings.

"You know you come from a family of writers."

"It skipped a generation, Mom edits romance novels. You're the last writer in our family."

Mrs. Tuesday's smiled at Mila's typical teenage deprecation of her mother's accomplishments. "Your mother has won industry awards for superior editing. And your great aunts were very important writers."

Her granddaughter sighed at the reiteration of well-worn territory, "I know Grandma."

"You should get to know them better."

"Their books haven't been published in years," her granddaughter countered. "Even the library archives don't have them."

"Your mother says you haven't come out to the house in a month and when she calls you're always out."

Mila shrugged. "Momma's not the same. Have you noticed?"

"Yes, it seems to have skipped a generation," Mrs. Tuesday said.

"What do you mean?"

"Things fall apart with age." Mrs. Tuesday looked toward the window on the other side of the room. "In some people it happens sooner than in others. Bodies, minds, some before their time."

"Grandma," her granddaughter reached out and gently placed a hand over hers, "We've taken her to a doctor, they think it might be early onset Alzheimer's."

Mrs. Tuesday nodded. "Is that what they call it? My Aunt's mind began to disintegrate when she was about your mother's age. I always thought it was because of the war. Now, the same is happening to my daughter, your mother, but without benefit of a war."

She shook her head at the unfairness of it all, how gladly she would trade places with her daughter, and to erase some of her own memories would be a blessing.

Mrs. Tuesday picked up the journals, flipped through one and then the other.

"This was written by my Aunt Natalie. It is her record of the last part of World War Two. The other journal is Anna's. Both will tell you about their lives as

writers. I've translated both journals for you." She handed another stack of typed pages to her granddaughter, "And this is a story that Aunt Natalie wrote during our last days together."

Her granddaughter shuffled through the pages, "How is this supposed to help me?"

Mrs. Tuesday clasped her granddaughter's hand and gave it a gentle squeeze. "I want you to see that others have gone through what your mother now faces. How you deal with it, is up to you, these journals will show you what others did."

"What about the envelope?" Mila asked.

Mrs. Tuesday looked but did not touch it, "One last bit of business I must attend to. I'm leaving tomorrow."

After her granddaughter left, Mrs. Tuesday went to her bedroom, put her suitcase on her bed, and began to pack. She hadn't been back in over seventy years. Now that the envelope had arrived, now that the end of her life was in sight, she was finally free to go home.

Not here, not this city where she'd lived since the war, hoped for years, given up hope, married, bore a child, made a career, grown old, this city had never felt like home.

Budapest was where she'd felt truly loved and now she would return. It was ridiculous to go at this time of year, but she didn't have the luxury of putting off the trip until summer.

She walked back into the living room and placed a thick white envelope addressed to her granddaughter on the coffee table. It contained a letter appointing her as the executor of Mrs. Tuesday's will, and provided instructions for the disposition of her belongings.

Mrs. Tuesday wasn't concerned with the fate of the furnishings; they suited her husband's tastes more than her own. However, she wanted her granddaughter to have the journals, both the Aunts' and the volumes Mrs. Tuesday had written herself over the years.

She had written detailed notes to her granddaughter on where she would be able to find her thoughts on editing and the writing process. She hoped they would encourage her to use the material in the journals in her own work. Perhaps then the legacy of their lives would live on.

When everything was finished, Mrs. Tuesday went to bed. She poured a glass of water from the carafe on the nightstand and swallowed the pills the doctor had prescribed. She set her alarm and climbed beneath the covers, but left the light on. Her gnarled fingers gently smoothed the blanket around her and she picked up a book of poems, but did not open them, letting the book gently rest on her chest. As she waited for sleep, she thought of Budapest and the war.

Chapter One

Budapest, Hungary

World War Two

"I can't sleep, Nana."

Mila's luminous skin glowed in the circle of light. Her young face was as innocent as the antique German porcelain doll I'd bought for her when she was a child. Long, dark lashes shaded her blue, almond-shaped eyes.

I opened the door that I'd just been ready to close shut, entered her bedroom, and settled into an overstuffed chair. With a sigh and a smile, I attempted to mask my anxiety. Lamplight silhouetted Mila's face in a halo of pale yellow, adding golden highlights to the dark curls, which fanned out across her pillow.

The book she held created a shadow across her

chest, making the pink roses on her nightgown glow and float among the tendrils of her long, dark hair. In the five years that Mila had lived here, there were few nights when I did not find her tucked beneath her comforter with a book to carry her to sleep.

Children's books have provided me with my job and my reputation. When Mila first arrived, I placed this chair next to her bed so I could read my stories to her. Over the years, the chair remained. I wrote more books, and read each one to Mila until she outgrew them. In time, she began to read the novels she found in my study, but the ritual of discussing books together before bed continued. Even during these years of war.

She propped the book against her chest and watched me expectantly. "You're coming with us, aren't you?"

"Of course." I turned from her gaze and smoothed the edge of the comforter, hoping this would be her only question.

"And Aunt Anna?" Mila's eyes searched my face for signs of deception.

"Yes, she seems to understand."

"But she forgets things so quickly," Mila added uneasily. "You know what she's like when she becomes confused."

"We'll sort it out in the morning." I folded my hands in my lap and leaned back in the chair. "She'll come if I ask her to."

"Mom's worried she'll slow us down."

"She said that to you?" My voice tightened as I finally looked into her eyes.

Mila broke our shared look first. "I overheard Mom and Bela in the kitchen before supper."

"I'll make sure that Anna reaches the station on time. We all will."

With that, we sat among the shadows of the bedroom. Neither of us wanted to discuss our complicated home life. My younger sister, Ilona, and her husband, Bela, resented me taking care of my twin sister, Anna. A year ago, Anna had moved in with us. She had been a poet in residence at the university, but a nervous breakdown made it impossible for her to continue living alone.

Mila began again. "When I try to talk to

Momma she snaps at me."

"She's probably just concerned about the arrangements for our trip," I offered.

"Sometimes she looks over at Bela before answering me."

"Bela's a difficult man."

"I think she's afraid he might leave without her. Would he do that, Nana?"

"No. He wouldn't leave without her."

I rubbed my hands down the length of my wool skirt to warm them. Despite the clanking radiators sitting like plump cats hissing and spitting against the bedroom walls, the room resisted warmth.

I disliked my younger sister Ilona's taste in men. She had no problem using hypochondria as an excuse against any form of housework or childrearing labors, and she'd picked her husbands accordingly. Men who were willing to care for her in exchange for total control of her movements and her affections—jealous masters.

Because of Ilona's character, and the low wages Bela received as a legal clerk, they'd come to live with me after my husband died. They insisted they were concerned about me living alone, although I knew my spacious apartment was a greater priority to them than my welfare.

I lived in a large, three-bedroom apartment, in the center of Budapest, and continued to use the master bedroom that I'd shared with my husband, Max, which still held his clothes and the familiar reminders of our life together. Mila slept in one of the two smaller bedrooms, and my sister Anna occupied the other. Ilona and Bela felt those bedrooms were too small for them, so when they realized I was not going to relinquish the room I had shared with my husband, they claimed the living room as the only space large enough to accommodate them comfortably.

As a result, my study became both a library and a living room, although the dining room and kitchen remained as they were when my husband and I lived alone. I maintained a fragile truce with Ilona and endured the angry outbursts of her husband in order to keep Mila near. She was an inquisitive and beautiful young girl—the daughter

I'd always wanted.

"What are you reading?" I gestured toward her book, hoping old habits would bring comfort and distract us from our separate worries.

"Aunt Anna's poems," Mila said, turning the cover toward me. "I can't believe that she wrote these words."

"Before her illness, Anna was a brilliant poet with an enormous talent for making the mundane extraordinary. She was a remarkable woman. She still is."

"I wish I could talk to her about the poems," Mila said.

"Try," I said. "There are moments when she still understands a great deal."

Mila pushed herself up in the bed and leaned toward me. "What does she remember?"

"For her, the poems that were written a decade ago are the freshest in her mind. That's some of her best work. She can still tell you exactly what she was trying to achieve in each line. Ironically, it's her inability to process what she did yesterday, or a moment ago, that keeps her from creating. It's sad, because she has more to say."

Mila leaned back against the pillows and chewed her lip. "Does she realize what's happening to her?"

I took Mila's hand in mine and gently squeezed it. "She knows."

A year ago, Anna handed me a stack of leather-bound books. The journals contained Anna's notes on poems that she had struggled through, political skirmishes at the university, and embarrassing details on her love life.

Anna asked me to edit and publish them for her. It was one of the first things she'd asked for when the doctor concluded that her delusional bouts would become more frequent. She wanted a testimony—something to remain as her identity slipped away.

I began working on them when my own writing stalled. I was piqued, discomfited, but also touched by what I read. In the long, sloping lines of revelation that covered the pages of her journals, I realized a depth to her I'd never imagined.

"How long will she recognize us, Nana?"

"I hope forever."

There are some things an adolescent girl like Mila should not have to learn too quickly—like the cruel irony that dementia would steal the talent that was Anna's greatest strength. I shook my head. No, that was the least of it. I needed to protect Mila from greater dangers than irony.

Chapter Two

Outside our windows, four floors above the street, the March wind moaned. The windows rattled and whistled softly as cold air seeped through cracks in the warped, wooden frames. The streets were unusually quiet. Even at this hour, Budapest should have been over-run with the sounds of the city. Now, there were no cars on the road or pedestrians making their way home from the opera house or the cafe. What a stark contrast to the celebrations held just days before.

On the fifteenth, the National Opera premiered *Petofi* to coincide with Hungary's national holiday. The Regent Horthy and his wife attended the event, and there was a shared opinion that this was an excellent omen. So many happy memories belonged in that hall.

Then, in the past two days, the lightness and hope vanished. The streets were alive with rumor and fear. It became clear that we would be drawn into the same hellish pit that had swallowed our neighbors. Budapest was the last morsel for the Nazis to devour before their own demise.

For years, we had remained remarkably untouched by the war. Hungary had made a pact with Germany, more to their economic benefit than ours, of course. In exchange, lands that had been taken from us during the First World War had been returned, and we were mollified. Then the tide turned. The Allies on one side and the Russians on the other were finally weakening Germany's stranglehold on Europe. As the noose tightened, the Germans had become more brutal. Bela told us of rumors that our government was secretly in negotiations with the Allies. As a result, Hitler had ordered his troops to invade Hungary, punishing us like ungrateful children.

An uneasy calm fell over the city. It was as if we were playing a dangerous game of hide-and-seek. People watched one another, no longer sure who to trust. We heard about what happened in Poland. Our government seemed more likely to aid the enemy than us.

Mila's voice brought me back into the room. "Did you ever write poetry?"

"Many years ago," I smiled, shaking off a painful memory.

"You haven't read anything to me lately. Are you working on anything new?"

"No." How to explain that knowing children were being separated from their parents and taken away to labor camps left me with little motivation to write imaginative stories. To lull innocents? To suggest that the world we had brought them into was fair and just? What point would a work of fantasy be in times of such horror? "People just don't seem interested in buying children's books right now," I said.

"You haven't stopped writing, have you?"

I bowed my head and considered my empty hands. "I have nothing to write about right now."

"When the war is over? Perhaps, when we get to Switzerland, when we are safe, you will write again?"

"Yes, when we are safe." I leaned over and gently kissed her forehead before blowing out the candle. Mila was my greatest source of inspiration. We had spent Sundays taking the tram to the zoo or the city park to rowboats on the pond. How could I write when she was in danger? How I wished I could attach the four posts of her bed to a hot air balloon and send her sailing through the night sky, across the ocean, to safety.

"Nana, what if the Germans arrive before we get to the train?"

I reached over and brushed the hair from her eyes. "I believe we still have a little time."

Mila turned to the window and flinched at the sound of distant gunfire.

"We'll leave before they get here," I promised.

"Do you really think we can?" Mila turned to look at me. "Everyone will need to get on that train. Is there enough room for all of us?"

"There will be enough room," I assured her. "We have tickets."

After saying goodnight to Mila, I passed the

dining room on the way to my study. The door was ajar, and I noticed Bela and Ilona whispering to one another. When they saw me, they stopped talking and Ilona turned away flushed with embarrassment, as if she'd been caught.

"Is everything ready for tomorrow?" I asked from the doorway.

Ilona pushed by me without making eye contact and quickly left the room.

Bela's cheeks burning bright from alcohol and indignation, growled, "You sneak around listening to conversations that are none of your business."

I didn't reply, only shook my head and continued to my study to drink coffee and write. Although this wasn't an ordinary night, I felt comfort in keeping with my nightly ritual of writing. Bela followed.

He was of medium height, with a stocky build and a handlebar moustache that seemed to fit with his monstrous demeanor. He was crude and unkempt, and his clothes always looked a size too small. Buttons strained against the girth of his stomach; his pants were wrinkled and the cuffs worn from age and neglect. I couldn't imagine what Ilona saw in him.

"Would you like a cup?" I asked, pouring one for myself. With engraved silver tongs, I dropped a lump of sugar into my cup.

"No." He shook his head, and made no move to come closer. I shrugged my shoulders and carried the cup across the room.

"Do you have our tickets?" I placed the cup on the table next to my chair, leaned over, and picked up the journal and pen that I'd left open on the seat.

"We get them tomorrow, at the train station."

"At the last minute?"

Noticing Bela's stupid, indignant face, I felt exasperated. He snorted and placed his hands on his hips as if meeting my challenge. Whatever drink he'd already consumed this evening magnified his belligerence.

The veins in his throat stood out like ropes. "I gave the man a deposit, but I need the rest of the money. The tickets are expensive."

"The despicable get rich by preying on the

desperate." I lowered myself into the chair, not taking my eyes from him.

"And the rich prey on everyone." Bela sneered. "What do you know of the real world?"

"I want to meet this ticket seller." I took a sip of coffee and watched his reaction.

He turned away from me and walked toward the window. "You'll meet him tomorrow."

"No. Tonight."

I put down the cup of coffee and took up my journal. I needed to keep my hands moving so that their shaking wouldn't be visible.

Bela stopped and stared at me, his forehead slick with sweat.

"That's not possible."

I flattened the pages with my fingers and read the previous day's entry, not seeing the words. "If he wants the money badly enough, he'll come."

He moved closer, stopping in front of my chair, his hands bunched in fists held at his side. He leaned over me and I recoiled from the stink of booze and his cheap Turkish cigarettes. "And if I can't find him?"

mrs. tuesday's departure

"I won't give you the money you need." I watched as the look of surprise on Bela's face turned to rage. Our eyes locked in mutual defiance.

Bela stormed out of the room. I heard him give directions to Ilona. The slamming of the front door shook the walls.

I let out a long breath, closed my eyes, and rested my head against the back of the chair. I closed my journal and clasped my hands together. Bela was right. I was ill prepared to handle these matters.

I opened my eyes and stood. On the bookcase, a china box still contained remnants of my husband's favorite pipe tobacco. The green velvet chair across from my desk was where I would find him in the hours between dinner and bedtime.

In the last days of his life, softly snoring, his book closed, his body weak and ravaged by cancer, Max seemed to fade into the down-filled cushions. I would come to his side, sit on the arm of the chair and wait until he would wake. He'd smile, put his arm around my waist, and pull me down for a kiss. He was twenty years older than me— shocking to my parents when I'd first brought him home.

I walked to the window. On the sidewalk below, Bela spoke to someone and then lit a cigarette, with blue smoke creating an unpleasant halo around his head. He crossed the street, stole a glance up at my window, and hurried down the block.

Max told me on many occasions of what he'd experienced in Russia. To teach me, so that I'd be prepared, he said. I'd always shaken him off; secure in the world that we'd created together, believing he would be able to protect me. Although, in the years since his death, I spent many nights struggling to remember his words.

How had we come so far? My childhood held fond memories of baking rich walnut rolls with our housekeeper. Of hiding under the heavy wooden kitchen table while Anna, with arms outstretched and eyes closed, counted down from ten to one.

How could I pack a lifetime into a small suitcase? Should I pack the precious silver or my jewelry, to sell or barter for housing and food? Do I leave behind the books that I wrote, the journals I kept, and the photos of those I've loved and who are now gone? They are my only tangible reminders. Do I find space for the tweed jacket that still carries the sweet smell of my husband's Latakia tobacco? The things that are invaluable to my heart hold no currency where we are going.

I walked across the room and turned into the hallway just as Ilona stepped out of Mila's room and closed the door behind her. She brushed a tear from her eye and then looked stricken upon seeing me. She ran her long, slender fingers through her faded red hair and tugged the loose tendrils into her chignon.

"Is Mila asleep?" I asked.

"Almost."

"She's worried about tomorrow," I said, turning back toward my study. I paused at the entrance, resting my hand on the doorknob. "I hope you were able to reassure her."

"How could you do this to Bela?"

I turned to look at my sister. "Do what?"

"Embarrass him like this." She clutched her arms against her bony chest as if she were trying to warm herself through the layers of clothes she wore.

I walked back to the window and gazed down at the street. "Max told me what people are capable of."

"Max isn't here. Bela will take care of everything."

"Bela's not Max."

"But he's my husband." Ilona paced the floor, shoulders hunched, head bent into her chest like a small bird. "He's the man in this household; therefore, he makes our decisions."

"For you, maybe," I said. "Not for me."

Ilona walked across the room and grabbed my sleeve. "He's all I have."

I placed my hand over hers. "Ilona, sometimes you are better alone than with someone who..."

Ilona wrenched her hand from my grasp. "I need him."

"Your daughter needs you," I said.

"And she needs a father. If you push him away, then what will we have?"

"You are all that she needs."

"I need Bela."

I grabbed her shoulders, "No, Ilona."

Her eyes widened as my fingers pressed into her arms and then she tore herself away.

"I can't do it alone. I need a man who will care for me."

"You can take care of yourself."

"I can't." Her narrow features were pulled taut. "I won't."

"Do you know that your daughter is afraid Bela will leave here without her?"

Ilona clutched her hands and quickly walked to the other side of the room. "She only complains because you've poisoned her against us."

"Did Bela tell you that?"

"He understands how I've been trapped."

"Trapped?" I asked, startled. "Who has trapped you? Me? Your daughter?"

"Yes," she screeched. "All of you!"

It often seemed like Ilona and Mila had exchanged roles. Ilona was only eighteen when she gave birth to Mila, and from day one Ilona treated her as a nuisance. One that threatened to ruin the shape of her breasts or the curve of her hips.

As soon as it was possible, Ilona and her husband were at it again, staying out all night in clubs and casinos. Ilona rationalized it as the only way she could keep him interested, but I think she enjoyed escaping their responsibilities as much as he did. When her first husband left her for another woman, Ilona blamed Mila. Then she quickly found and married Bela.

"Are we all responsible for your unhappiness?"

"You know what I'm talking about."

"No." I shook my head, not wanting to hear the litany of her complaints.

"Everything was used up on you and Anna."

"You were loved by all of us."

"Not the way you loved each other," she said. "I know the difference."

"Ilona," I sighed. "How many people will you blame for your failures?"

Nevertheless, deep down, I acknowledged some truth in her accusations. Ilona had been born ten years after Anna and me. We were little blonde dolls in the eyes of our parents, and they showered us with toys. We responded with a keen intelligence that delighted them. By comparison, Ilona's birth had been difficult, her infancy marked by colic, her childhood marked by mischief.

Even her frizzy, auburn hair highlighted her difference. We'd been brought up in the Catholic Church, but Ilona had married a Jew. This meant that under the laws instituted by the Nazis, not only was her husband in jeopardy, so was she—and so was Mila.

We turned in unison at the sound of footsteps hurrying down the hall toward us. Bela entered my study followed by a young stranger.

"I've brought him." Bela jerked his thumb back. Behind him stood a young man, perhaps fifteen, cap in hand, nervously twisted like a rag. His black hair was slicked back, his shirt dirty and pants hung loosely from his frame. His eyes gave away years of bitter experience.

"Where are the tickets?"

The boy squared his shoulders and regarded

me defiantly. I could imagine how Bela had described me. "I don't have them."

"Why not? Where are they?"

"I can't get them until he," the young boy gestured to Bela, "gives me the money I need."

The negotiations had begun. I gestured toward a chair. "Sit down."

The boy remained standing. "Please." I added.

He glanced around the room and then took a seat closest to the door. I poured a cup of coffee and handed it to him with a small plate of biscuits.

I watched him savor what I knew was the best coffee he'd had in these days of black-market chicory. I needed to establish our roles. Coffee, his hunger, this room, the ancient Oriental rug he scraped his muddy shoes against—these were just props. Bela and Ilona stood in the doorway as if watching a show.

"Where will you get the tickets?" I took a sip from my cup and made a show of enjoying the rich taste before placing the cup back in its saucer. "It's been impossible to get a seat on any train going to Switzerland."

"I have a friend at the train station," the boy said, not meeting my eyes.

He was lying. There were no friends now, only business associates. He took one cookie from the plate, and then stuffed the rest into his coat pocket.

I watched his eyes roam the area as if appraising the value of the paintings or the plates arranged on the shelves between the rows of books. Good, I thought, fighting a sense of violation. "Why not use the tickets for yourself or your family?"

"I don't need to escape." He straightened the lapels of his jacket with an air of nonchalance. Then he leaned back in the chair as if this domain was no longer mine, but his. "I'm not a Jew."

"Neither am I." I smiled.

The smug look faded from his face.

He considered me, and then Bela, as if expecting an explanation. "You need to leave the country, right?"

"No one wants to remain in the middle of a war," I replied, drawing his attention back to me. In wartime, people seek information that might be useful. As such, we guarded our privacy like a precious commodity.

Bela interrupted. "It's her niece she's interested in saving."

Ilona's cheeks flushed in embarrassment, she pursed her lips as if a secret had escaped. I shook my head but offered no explanation.

"And don't forget that you are a Jew as well, Bela," I said.

Bela's mouth opened to respond, but Ilona grabbed his arm.

"Bela gave you a deposit," I said turning to the boy. "How much more do you need for five tickets?"

The ticket seller started to answer, but Bela stepped forward and cut him off. "The deposit covers only a quarter of the total price of the tickets."

I addressed the boy, "Will you meet us at the station tomorrow to give us the tickets?"

"Yes."

"What guarantee do we have that you'll be there?"

The boy shrugged his shoulders and smiled gamely. "You don't."

"Other than your desire to make a healthy profit."

"I have to feed my family."

"Your father?" I asked.

"In the army. My mother and sisters depend on me."

Another lie. Our eyes met and, with a tilt of his head and the faintest smile, he acknowledged my conclusion.

Ilona clutched Bela's arm. "Natalie, you ask too many questions."

I smiled at the boy. "I will rely on your greed."

I rose to signify the conversation's end. The boy nodded grimly and stood to leave.

Bela regarded me with contempt. "Are you satisfied?"

"When we have the tickets in our hands I will be."

"You see, Ilona, she's never pleased." Bela took her arm, "Let's go to bed."

Ilona paused at the threshold of the doorway,

with eyes filled with pain and something else. Anger, perhaps? Or was it victory?

Chapter Three

Under the circumstances, I found it hard to sleep. Eventually, my worried mind gave in to tiredness and I dozed off, only to be jolted awake by the sound of dishes splintering the silence. Like the battle scene from Wagner's *Ring Cycle*, Bela's baritone answered Anna's bewildered cry. From the darkness of my room, I rushed into a wall of light, squinting as I ran down the hallway toward the sound of my sister's voice.

Anna stood in the center of the kitchen wearing my late husband's faded woolen robe, so ridiculously large for her slender frame that she appeared to be a child playing dress up.

"It's not my fault, it's not my fault. The maid told me she would draw my bath before dinner."

"The maid's gone, and it's morning you crazy

woman," Bela roared.

"Who will run my bath?" My sister's arms waved uselessly at her sides. "I'm going to be late, Natalie." Her tousled blonde hair all but obscured her red-rimmed eyes that pleaded for an explanation.

"Get out of here!" Bela yelled. "We're not going to wait for you."

Anna froze in her tracks, oblivious to Bela's threat.

Bela pulled the tins off the shelves, looked through them, and tossed them away in anger. "Where did you put the money?"

"I gave you all the money I had."

"I know you keep a stash hidden somewhere around here."

My throat knotted as I pushed my way past him. My slippers crackled over shards of dishes. My sister's feet were bare, a small pool of blood formed halos around her toes like the petals of peonies. I winced as if the pain were mine.

In her image, I saw myself, deranged, helpless, and lost. "I'm here, Anna."

"My bath's not ready." My sister rocked back and forth in time to a slow, baleful moan rising from her chest. The slivers of plate that were cutting into her feet drew no reaction on her face.

"Damn it!" Bela, hollered. He elbowed us aside and went to the counter and began shoving food into a knapsack. "Get that bitch out of my way."

"Natalie, why won't he leave?" Anna glanced at me reproachfully. "Deliveries are supposed to be made before noon."

"Here, put on my slippers," I whispered, sliding them off. Anna's gaze swept toward me and then at her own bloodied feet, and her moaning rose to a piercing wail.

"Who cut my feet?" She wiped her feet back and forth in the blood, smearing it into an even wider circle. "Who cut me?"

"My God!" Ilona stood in the doorway clutching an over-stuffed suitcase. "We're going to miss the train."

Bela turned and held out his hand, silencing her. "Nothing will make us miss the train, Ilona. I promise."

"She'll get blood on the food," Ilona screeched.

"The blood is on the floor, not on the food!" I brushed the shards from the soles of Anna's feet and slipped my slippers on her feet.

"Ilona, put your case next to the door and wait there." Turning to me, Bela snapped, "You'll have to pack your own food. This knapsack will only hold enough for Ilona and me."

I straightened up and sent a withering gaze at Bela. "Just don't forget to find space in that bag for Mila's portion."

"Mila can pack her own bag. She's old enough to do that."

"So is your wife."

He shrugged and shoved another container of tinned meat into the knapsack. "She needs more help than Mila."

I watched him, mesmerized by his greed and single-mindedness. It was clear that he planned to stash as much food as possible in a sack he had no intention of sharing. "For God's sake, Bela, there are other people in this family."

A jar of pickles crashed to the floor, its

pungent liquid creating a morbid watercolor as it washed over the splotches of blood. Anna cringed. I put my arm around her shoulders as she buried her head against my chest.

Bela grabbed the knapsack and pushed past us with a parting shot. "We're leaving."

Silence fell. I surveyed the damage and fought the compulsion to clean up the mess. Carefully, I made my way across the room, guiding my sister and wincing as shards of porcelain cut into the soles of my feet.

"Nana?" Mila appeared in the doorway.

"Mila, come and pack your food." I lifted a sack toward her and gestured toward the cupboards.

"I did, last night." She took the bag from my hands. "I'll pack some food for you."

"Take your bag to the door. Your parents are getting ready to leave."

Mila reached for Anna. "Let me help you."

"Take Anna to her room and see if you can get her to change into her street clothes. I'll be there in a minute."

Looking at the shelves, I saw what I already knew, that there was little food left to pack. Bela had taken the coffee, sugar, bread and salami, and anything else he could cram into his knapsack. There was almost nothing left. I could do no more than take a tin of sardines and a jar of pickled cabbage. I pulled them off the shelf and shoved them into a paper sack. Perhaps if we were lucky, we'd be able to buy food on the train or in a village along the rail.

"Nana!" Mila's voice echoed down the hallway.

I grabbed the meager bag of food and hurried to Anna's bedroom. My sister sat on the edge of her bed wearing a navy blue silk ball gown that I hadn't seen in years. The buttons on the back of the dress were undone, with the outline of Anna's spine and ribs pushed against her translucent skin like the teeth of a gaping zipper.

Bunched around her waist were the bottoms of her flannel pajamas, incongruously forming a pink and white rosebud against the silk of the gown. Mila crouched helplessly on the floor, vainly attempting to wrestle stockings and boots onto Anna's feet.

"She's doesn't understand. She insists that she's going to the opera with Deszo. Is he actually coming for her?"

"No, of course not."

Deszo was a professor of economics at the university where Anna taught. He broke off their affair and returned to his wife when Anna's behavior became too erratic to manage.

"How will we get her to the train station?"

"By entering the play in her head," I said, stepping over to relieve Mila. "Anna, there's snow on the ground; you'll have to wear your boots."

Anna sniffed. "My boots will look ridiculous with my gown."

"Carry your shoes and put them on once you're inside the theater or they'll be ruined." I knelt in front of her and began replacing the blue silk shoes with leather boots.

Anna kicked me away. "Why are you hurrying me? I still have to do my face!"

"You don't have time to do your face," I

sighed. "Deszo will be here any minute."

Anna jumped up and raced to her vanity. "You should have told me he was going to be early!"

Staring at her reflection in the mirror she rubbed vicious slashes of rouge across her pale cheeks. She grabbed a lipstick and traced an irregular shape around her lips. Her hands raked through her tangled hair.

I bundled my sister's coat around her shoulders and steered her towards the door. "Mila, can you grab the suitcase over there?"

"But where are your things, Nana?"

"Packed with Anna's," I replied. "Can you manage our case with yours? Just until we get downstairs to the taxi."

We stumbled down the hall, Mila clutching our suitcase, Anna fighting to free herself from my grasp. The front door stood open, the two suitcases next to it had vanished.

"They've left without us!" Mila ran out on to the stairwell and leaned over the railing. The echo of the heavy steel front door closing two floors below rang through the stairwell and ended in silence.

I felt we should do our best to catch up, so we grabbed what we could and dashed out.

~*~

"Nana, we're not going to make it!"

Turning from where I was desperately trying to hail a taxi, I watched my young niece run into the street.

"Mila get back on the sidewalk with Anna!"

Tires squealed, and a horn blasted. While trying to follow Mila, Anna stepped into the path of a car. The front fender grazed her, spinning her in slow motion. For an instant, I shared her helpless vertigo as the world spun before my eyes, and sky and buildings and pavement swirled around my head like a tumbling house of cards.

She fell with all the pageantry of a well-dressed bundle of sticks, arms outstretched, the blue silk of her ball gown parachuted up and over her head, revealing spindly legs covered by striped flannel pajama bottoms. She landed on the road in a heap of colorful fabric. My poor, delusional sister, dressed for a night at the opera on the morning that held our last chance to escape from the Nazis.

I rushed to her side. Mila knelt next to Anna, wiping blood from her forehead while I cradled Anna's head in my lap.

The driver of the car jumped out and shouted, "I didn't see her coming! She walked out in front of me."

"Anna, where does it hurt?" My hands frantically groped through the yards of fabric surrounding her legs to test for broken bones.

"Why don't you look where're you're going!" yelled the driver over the blaring horns of the stalled traffic.

"Look at my dress!" Anna moaned. "I'll have to go back upstairs to change."

"Your dress is fine," I made an effort to brush off the dirt.

"Deszo will notice the stain on the skirt."

"He's too much a gentleman," I assured her.

Anna winced as she tried to raise herself. "My head hurts."

Looking up, I yelled at the driver of the car. "We have to get to the train station. You have to help us."

"Why?" He threw his arms up in the air. "Because this crazy woman ran in front of my car?"

"Yes," I yelled. "Please, we have to catch a train."

"There's no way you can get to the train station in this traffic."

"Please help us," I begged. "We have to leave."

Cursing, he slammed his fist on the hood. "Get in the car."

Mila and I lifted Anna to her feet and helped her into the back seat of the car. The driver pulled back into traffic, and lurched around a corner, nearly sideswiping a delivery truck attempting the same corner from the opposite direction.

"Nana, how much time do we have?" Mila asked.

I checked my watch. Worry shook my hands. "Ten minutes."

"Ten minutes until the train leaves?" The driver craned his neck around to look at me.

"Yes."

He shook his head, hunched over the steering wheel, the edge of his dirty wool coat rubbed against the side of his cap. "No chance. You'll never make it."

Still, he accelerated into traffic as if inspired by the impossibility of our plight, and then jammed on his brakes as another car swerved in front of him. He retaliated by cutting off the car in turn, gesturing wildly and swearing oaths.

"What's wrong with this driver?" Anna asked. "This isn't the way to the Opera House."

"Ignore her!"

He swore again, and the car leapt. As we turned the corner, I saw a sliver of our beloved Danube and the Parliament building, which sat on the river's edge like a plump wedding cake. I shivered as I noticed the German tanks that circled it like a line of hungry rats.

Mila looked out the front window. "Nana, Momma wouldn't let the train leave without us."

"Of course not," I said.

"She said we could take a later train." Mila turned to me, her enormous blue eyes revealed her doubt more profoundly than her words.

"Of course." I shot the driver a warning glance as he stared at me through the rear view mirror.

"Anna how are you feeling?" I asked.

"I have an awful headache."

"What were you thinking, walking out into the street like that?"

"That's where you were." she smiled up at me.

I leaned over, kissed her forehead, and gently brushed my fingers across her bruised cheek.

"We're going to miss the first curtain," Anna said. "I hope Deszo will wait for us."

The traffic piled up and finally stopped. The driver slammed the steering wheel. "Lady there's no way I can get you any closer than this."

We were losing time. The train station was three blocks ahead.

"Mila, grab our bags, we'll have to run the rest of the way." I opened the door and helped Anna to her feet.

I handed the driver a wad of bills. "Thank you."

He smiled sadly, "Good luck."

Chapter Four

We hurried through the stalled cars and throngs of pedestrians. Three unaccompanied children running against the current surrounded us. With ragged, smiling faces, one stretched out a hand while another surreptitiously tried to find an entrance into a pocket or purse.

Anna cried out as a teenage boy grabbed her coat. I slapped him away. Instinctively I clutched the lapels of my coat shut. Shoved from side to side, we slowly made our way onward. Pushed out into the road we moved between stalled cars.

Regaining the sidewalk, I clutched Anna as her feet slipped on a patch of worn shiny ice and her legs collapsed beneath her. Mila was steps ahead of us, looking back from moment to moment, urging us to keep up with her. Finally, we crossed the last street before the train station.

It took a moment for my eyes to adjust to the poorly-lit gloom of the cavernous main hall. Our shoes slid against the slick marble floors. We stumbled over suitcases and bags tied together haphazardly with twine.

Old women fleeing the terror in the villages sat in a stupor clutching their grandchildren in one hand and their meager belongings in another. Men in ill-fitting military uniforms shifted listlessly from one foot to another, waiting for orders. Beggars, limbs missing, were propped against the steps like discarded luggage. We slogged our way through the main hall toward the stairs that lead to the train platforms. To our left, we passed a waiting area shrouded in darkness, and where row upon row of benches were crowded with silent, vacant souls.

"Nana," Mila yelled pointing to a sign overhead. "The train is on track three."

"See if you can find your mother," I shouted. "And get on the train."

Mila hesitated.

"Go!" I shouted. "We'll meet you there."

mrs. tuesday's departure

The crowd swallowed Mila, and I prayed that she would get on the train. Even though her success would cause our separation.

Clinging to one another in grey-cloaked clusters were those who had decided security was hiding in direct sight. Others ran from one place to another, imagining help right around the corner. I grabbed my sister's face, and our eyes met. "You must help me. We've got to get to the train platform."

For a moment, the clouds in her eyes parted and lucidity beamed through.

"Yes, let's go."

We locked arms. Swept into the current of bodies pouring toward the entrance to the tracks, we struggled to keep up.

On the tracks, a blast of frigid air washed away the fetid stink of the terminal. The noise level rose to a roar. The mob surged with the desperate energy of passengers on a sinking ship.

Shouts from train conductors fought with the outraged claims of passengers without tickets. Fights broke out as people clawed and shoved their way onto to overcrowded trains. Above all of this, the monstrous hissing of engines and the bone crushing scraping of metal against metal heralded the trains' departure.

I searched the crowded platform. My anger and fear mounted at the impossible task of holding onto Anna while watching for Mila.

I grabbed a passing conductor. "Where's the train to Geneva?"

"Ahead on the left," he shouted. "It's leaving."

I grabbed Anna's arm, using my shoulder to force a gap in the throng.

"Mila! Ilona!" My entreaties were swallowed by the cries of my neighbors. I saw the train and continued pushing until I reached an open space just along the edge of the platform. I had to avoid falling onto the tracks, but ahead, I could see Mila arguing with a conductor as she tried to get onto the train. I used all my strength to push toward her.

"My mother has my ticket!" Mila pleaded. She attempted to push past the conductor. "Let me on and I'll get the ticket from her."

I dragged Anna along with me until she

refused to keep up. I dropped her hand and ran on without a word or a look backward.

The conductor shoved Mila back onto the platform. "No ticket, no entrance. This train is full."

The train shuddered, lurched forward and back. Undecided, it paused as if waiting for further orders. There was a loud roar of steel and steam and I watched in horror as it started to inch forward. Mila noticed, and her attempts grew more desperate.

"Please let me on." Mila desperately skipped sideways to keep pace with the train. "My mother has my ticket."

Her gaze swept the length of the train and then she sprinted. She stopped halfway down the car and then started trotting to keep pace with the slowly moving train.

Mila pounded on a window of the train, screaming, "Momma!"

The window opened, and Ilona leaned out. "Mila, how did you get here?"

Mila reached up and grasped her mother's fingers. "Momma, give me my ticket."

"I don't have it."

They were moving too fast now. I ran to catch up, spellbound by the macabre drama.

Ilona yelled, "Take her home. It's too late!"

"Why, Momma?"

Ilona glared at me and then at Mila.

"Tell her Ilona! Tell her!" I shouted. "There never were more than two tickets!"

The wind whipped the hair across Mila's twelve-year-old face as it crumbled in despair. "Momma, please don't leave me."

Ilona's face was pained but defiant. My stomach churned with shame. Was this my younger sister? Was she raised in the same family as Anna and me? She glanced at her daughter and then closed the window and turned away.

Mila stopped. Her arms fell to her sides. She stood helplessly watching the train as it gathered speed. "But Momma…I love you."

~*~

I rushed to Mila's side, my heart pierced by the

vacant, questioning look on her face. I gathered her into my arms. Her body was limp, cold, and weighted against mine. Over the top of her head, I saw Anna standing in the midst of the crowd, holding our suitcase. Our eyes met, and she shook her head. I wondered, and then knew from the look in her eyes, that despite her bouts of delusion, she understood what just happened.

I buried my face in the sweet, tangled mass of Mila's hair. We stood together, crying as the station continued to throb and swarm around us. I knew everything had changed. I knew things would get worse before they got better.

The train had been my last hope of getting Mila to safety. I stared at the empty track and knew that I would never see Ilona again.

"Why did she leave without me?" Mila whispered.

We swam against the current along the train platform, and up the stairs to the main hall, pushing our way through the crowds still encamped in the terminal. With our heads down, we climbed the steps leading from this level of

Dante's hell and pressed through the heavy doors leading out to the street.

The sun broke through the clouds, and we shielded our eyes. It was the first real sunlight we'd seen in weeks. The brightness seemed surreal. We walked for a few blocks, regaining our bearings. Mila's breathing steadied, though she continued to stumble along, head down, allowing us to guide her. Under the weight of my hand placed on the back of her coat, I could feel the sobs that had racked her chest were subsiding. Anna was silent.

Within a few blocks of the station, we managed to elbow our way onto a crowded tram. The steamed windows made it difficult to see the familiar blocks as we re-traced our path home. I leaned over to place our bags on the floor by my feet, and a stout woman next to me shoved me back with a curse. I realized how little our concerns mattered to anyone else.

I knew why earlier generations once believed that the sun circled the earth. Because, in our limited imaginations, that is how we live our lives. I understand how crimes could be committed in full view. That myopia, I feared, would be our downfall.

We got off the tram a block from our building and trundled up the steps to our apartment. The door stood open as if awaiting our return.

The light slanted eerily through the windows and across the floor, highlighting the fragments of shattered plates in the kitchen.

Walking down the hall to Mila's room, I glanced in to my study remembering the events of last night.

What could I have done differently?

It's true the situation seemed uncertain last night, but I still couldn't believe Ilona and Bela left without us. Their selfishness made my head burn with anger. I don't know what to do. I have no plan, and the worst part was knowing I promised Mila that everything would be alright.

Mila stood with her arms at her side as I took her coat off and unbuttoned her sweater. I had failed her. With all my precautions, I had not counted on a mother choosing to save her husband rather than her daughter.

"Put on your nightgown and get into bed," I said.

Anna tilted her head and nodded, smoothing Mila's hair. "It's the best place to cry."

Mila turned, and the briefest of smiles crossed her face, and then dissolved. I closed the shutters on each window to darken the room against the mid-day sunlight. I hoped she would sleep for a while, escape to a world of dreams. Anna and I left her room, gently closing the door behind us.

Anna followed me down the hall to the kitchen. We stood in the doorway and surveyed the damage. The cabinet doors were open, the shelves empty. The window over the sink flooded the room with muted light and cast shadows across the kitchen table, where a single jar of pickled beets still stood next to the empty pots for cream and sugar and dirty cups containing the dregs of last night's coffee.

"Who left the kitchen in such a state?" Anna asked. "Mother will be furious."

I looked at her and then at the wreckage. No use explaining that our mother had been dead for more than fifteen years. The events of this morning, I hoped, were just as forgotten. I stepped into the room and began to sweep the shards of broken crockery into a pile. There was nothing to do but sweep up and start again.

Chapter Five

"I need to go out for a while," I said.

Anna grabbed her coat and headed to the door. "Where are we going?"

"Stay here with Mila. I'm just going to the grocers." I took her coat and hung it on the hook near the door. "I won't be long. We need food. There's none left in the cupboard."

"You're coming back, aren't you?" Anna's face wrinkled with childish concern. I worried about leaving her alone, but I knew that the short trip would take too long if she came with me. I hated that the simplest tasks had become a choice of loyalty over practicality.

"I'll be back in a very short time."

"How long?"

I checked my watch and then the one on her

wrist, synchronizing the two. I tapped her wrist. "I'll be back in thirty minutes."

"When will you be back?" she asked again.

I sighed, "Soon."

"Will Deszo be with you?"

"I don't think so."

"No, I guess he wouldn't." She shrugged her shoulders.

Anna decided to go to her room. In her usual struggle with lucidity, she voiced both a desire to make the final act at the opera and the need to rest. As I watched her walk down the hall in her filthy ball gown, I thanked God for the rational moments she still had left, and shook my head knowing those moments grew more infrequent as her insanity claimed a wider territory.

I grabbed my purse and shoved the money that I'd tied around my neck into it. As much as I needed to go to the grocers to replenish our supply of food, I needed the time away from Anna and Mila even more, to sort out my thoughts.

Trudging downstairs, I wondered why I'd been so blind to Ilona's ruse. Passing by the door of the other apartment in the building, I wondered if I would be able to turn to my neighbors for help. Or if they could keep a secret.

I shook my head. Mourning the past or counting on the help of acquaintances would get me nowhere. I had one mission—to protect Mila. I leaned against the steel door and stepped back into the afternoon light and fresh air.

As the laws against Jews and those associated with them grew more severe, we decided to dismiss our housekeeper. It wasn't reasonable to expect someone with no ties to our family to keep secret the hiding of Jews in our home.

If it had been Marie, the loyal housekeeper we'd had during my years of marriage, she would still be with us, and trust would not be an issue. But as the war drew closer to our borders, she returned to her village to help her brother's family.

Since Marie's departure, I'd hired and fired another four housekeepers, for incompetence or suspected thievery. In years past, I would have overlooked a housekeeper who took some of our foodstuffs for her own kitchen, but as supplies grew more difficult to procure, I could no longer tolerate the loss of food that was becoming difficult to replace.

I made my way down the street to the small shop owned by Mr. Nyugati, and was surprised to find the metal gate drawn down in front of the doorway leading to his shop. I knocked and called out his name.

"We're closed," answered his wife. "Go away."

I yelled through the seams in the gate. "It's me, Natalie. Let me in. I just need a few things."

"We have no more food to sell."

"Please," I pleaded. "I'll take whatever you have."

I heard Mr. Nyugati arguing with his wife and then the gate rolled up halfway, and I quickly ducked under it and through the door.

It was dark and the air was warm inside the shop. As my eyes adjusted, I saw that Mrs. Nyugati had spoken the truth. The shelves were empty of all but a few cans.

"What happened?" I asked.

"The Arrow Cross soldiers were here this

morning. They came and took everything we had and didn't pay," Mrs. Nyugati complained.

"How could they?"

"They said we were selling to Jews," Mr. Nyugati replied. "So we were to be closed down. In the meantime, they would punish us by taking everything."

"You must report them!"

"To whom? The police? It's your kind that are getting us into trouble in the first place!"

"Be quiet woman," Mr. Nyugati warned.

"It's true!"

"The noose is getting tighter," he said. "Now anyone caught helping a Jew faces severe punishment." He gave me a knowing look.

"One of the men said he would pay us for names," Mrs. Nyugati leaned in and smiled.

"It's just me and Anna now. Ilona and her family are gone," I replied.

"When?" she asked.

I considered this little round woman whom I'd known all my life and was surprised by the change in her demeanor. When Mila was a child, she would come to this store, and Mrs. Nyugati would give Mila a handful of candy. "They left this morning."

"Not likely," Mrs. Nyugati sneered. "The borders are closed."

"They managed to get on the last train," I countered.

"Enough," Mr. Nyugati pushed his wife to the back of the store. After she left, he turned to me. "If they are in hiding, make sure it's not your apartment. They've begun to expand their searches."

"I promise, they are gone. But what will you do now?" I knew the small income they made from this store was barely enough to support them.

"I've sent my son out to talk with their commander," Mr. Nyugati sighed. His son had been denied service in the army as the result of a clubfoot. "I gave him the small amount of money I had, and he'll try to make a bribe that will allow us to re-open."

"Is there anything left that I can buy?" I walked down the aisle picking up the cans of vegetables. "I'll take whatever you have."

"Here, let me help you," Mr. Nyugati took my basket and began to fill it. He carried it behind the counter and reached beneath to pull out a loaf of bread, a short string of kielbasa, a wedge of cheese with bits of blue mold clinging to the edges, and a couple handfuls of potatoes.

"I greatly appreciate this," I opened my purse to pay him. "Will you be able to get more?"

"I don't know," he said. "And please go out the back way, along the alley. It's safer that way."

I followed him down the long corridor that bisected the storeroom and the stairway that led to the small apartment where they lived with their son, Stephen, and his wife and child.

He opened the door for me and surveyed the alleyway to be sure it was clear before stepping aside to let me pass.

"Can I come again?"

"It's not safe. I'll send my son to your apartment in a few days."

"Thank you, Mr. Nyugati." I said, as I looked into his eyes and pressed money into his hand.

mrs. tuesday's departure

Chapter Six

I hurried into the alleyway and heard the door shut behind my back. The passage was almost as dire as the store and stank of rubbish. I stepped gingerly around piles of rotting food and stifled a scream as a rat, shiny with filth, ran across my path.

At the end of the building, I stepped onto the sidewalk just as a troop of Arrow Cross soldiers crossed to the other side of the street.

The leader of the group screamed, "Halt!"

I jumped backwards into the shadow of the alley, my heart pounding as I pressed against the grimy, brick wall. I held my breath and strained to hold the basket in my shaking hands.

I was not their prey.

An old woman wearing a faded yellow star on

the breast of her coat stood three paces in front of them. She froze.

"Why are you on the street and not in the ghetto?"

I saw her flinch and offer her basket.

They laughed and knocked it out of her hands. "Show us your papers!"

She pointed to the yellow star on her coat and then began to fumble with her purse, searching to produce the documents.

"Who are you buying food for? Where are the rest of your family hiding?"

Sobbing, she denied their charges. They screamed at her calling her a "filthy, Jewish whore". They surrounded her, pushing and shoving her against the building. A young soldier raised his fist and brought it down. Her head snapped back against the blow and she stumbled, but remained upright.

Others passed by this scene with heads bowed, making a wide circle or crossing the street. Before the war, these thugs would have been banished like a pack of dogs.

Yet, no one uttered a word in protest as the soldiers joined their comrade in the beating. The woman slid to the pavement with her arms raised in vain defense against the rain of blows. Her pleas for mercy met with laughter and insults and steel-toed boots that punctured her stomach and broke her ribs.

My stomach churned in disgust. Dropping my basket of food, I pushed myself from the wall and ran across the street.

"Stop it! You'll kill her!"

I threw myself on top of the woman, holding her bleeding head in my arms. Her hands grasped the back of my coat as if she were drowning. Strong arms grabbed me, but I continued to scream as they threw me to the side.

My hands scraped against the concrete as I tried again to hold her in my arms. I felt the skin of my knuckles split. Still, I held her. My face pushed into the collar of her coat. I smelled the sweat of her fear mingled with my own. When I raised my face to hers, our eyes met. I looked into tired, brown eyes, creased with pain, not of this event, but of the years that preceded it.

"No," she whispered. "Go."

A young thug pulled me away. He threw me onto the sidewalk and I grabbed his leg to regain my balance. Instinctively, he swung the butt of his rifle, striking me in the face. As I slid into darkness, I heard someone calling my name.

Chapter Seven

I tried to get my bearings through the fog, but my vision clouded. I saw my husband's face, his serene gaze focused on my own. It was not the face he'd had when he died. This one was no longer ravaged by disease, thinned because he was no longer able to eat. These eyes were not lifeless, but vibrant and witty. In death, my husband had returned to the beauty of the days of our early marriage.

"How could they let an old woman be beaten?" I asked.

"Because she is not their old woman, Natalie," he soothed. "Why are you so naive?"

"Have we come to this?"

"This is only the beginning," he replied.

"I have to save Mila," I said. "Ilona has

abandoned her."

He nodded. "I know, but you must be more careful."

"Is this a dream?"

His eyes twinkled, and he smiled. "No, not really."

His eyes were fathomless. Like those of the old woman. "But you're not real."

His eyebrows rose in surprise, "Of course I'm real."

I searched for his hand. "Am I becoming like Anna?"

"You're stronger than you think." His breath was warm against my hand, his mouth as soft as an angel's wing.

"Take me with you," I begged.

Swallowed in a golden filmy haze, Max's face faded from my view. "No, not yet, my darling. Not yet."

"Come back!" I coughed, and reached into the emptiness— but found nothing.

Blinking back the throbbing in my skull, I slowly raised myself and slid up the wall. The sun had set below the buildings, casting long, gray shadows down the street. A man leaned over, helped me to my feet, and then scurried off before I could thank him.

"Max?"

My head swam with pain. I stumbled and then saw the old woman sprawled on the sidewalk. I knelt and touched her face. It was cold and lifeless and yet, people walked by, avoiding my stare.

Raising my head I whispered, "Dear God, have mercy on her soul and on ours for our sins."

Pushing myself up, I managed to cross the street to the alley. There, I found my basket of food untouched.

Somehow, I found my way home. Mila and Anna met me at the door. The fear on their faces turned to anger when they saw the bruise on my head.

Anna touched my cheek. "What happened?"

I handed Mila the basket of food as Anna took off my coat. "An accident," I replied.

"Who did this to you?" Mila demanded. "Were you robbed?"

"No, it was the soldiers."

"I heard their bull horn. They were announcing another curfew," she said. "I was coming to look for you."

The thought of Mila alone on the streets, confronted by the Arrow Cross, perhaps meeting the same fate as the old woman, was too much. Suddenly the full extent of the day's events caught up with me.

My eyes filled with tears, and I reached out for Mila's arm. "I need to sit down."

"You need dinner." Mila grabbed my arm and I leaned against her, resting my face on her head. Her hair was soft against my cheek, so soft. I turned and kissed the top of her head.

Anna came to my right, placed her arm around my waist, guided me to a chair and gently pushed me down into it. "Sit and I'll be right back." She hurried down the hall to the bathroom, and I could hear her rummaging through the cabinet.

"Mila, it's not safe for you to leave the apartment," I said. "We have to make arrangements to hide you. To get you to safety."

Mila placed the basket on the counter and began to take the food out. "I want to stay here with you."

I rubbed my head wearily. "Max said I should find someone to help us."

"Uncle Max?" Mila turned to me, and furrowed her brow in concern.

I saw the fear in her eyes and immediately recanted. "No, I'm confused. It was just a thought that occurred to me."

She shook her head, not ready to believe me. "We should call a doctor."

Anna came in and knelt by my side. With tender concern, she dabbed the bruise on my forehead with a cotton swab and antiseptic. I flinched at the burning sensation.

"I'm sorry, Natalie," Anna said. "Mila's right, we should call a doctor."

"No. I'll be fine. We can't invite anyone to come here. It's too dangerous. Just bandage it, Anna."

Anna's eyes met mine as she placed the bandage on the wound. "Tell us how this happened."

"I was stupid," I said. "Coming home from Mr. Nyugati's store, I saw an old woman being assaulted by the Arrow Cross. No one would help her."

"So you did."

"I tried," I sighed.

"And you got this for your efforts?"

"Yes," I said.

"What happened to the old woman?" Mila asked.

I remained silent. Anna shook her head. Mila persisted. "What happened to her?"

"It was too late to help her."

"They took her away?"

I shut my eyes, seeing the old woman's battered face before me. "When I woke up she was dead. They killed her. For what? Because her papers weren't in order. Because she was a Jew."

Mila turned back to the stove, but her body shuddered. I pushed myself up from the table and embraced her. "I'll just go to bed. We'll sort this out in the morning."

Exhausted, I went to my room and closed the door. I was too tired to bathe, so I shed my clothes, pulled on a nightgown and slipped between the covers. I longingly stared at the picture of Max that sat on my nightstand.

I picked up the heavy, silver frame and clutched it to my chest. I heard him sigh from the corner of the room, and I gently laid the frame on the pillow next to me. I turned on my side and let my fingers trace the edge of the sheets where he had lain next to me for years. "Come back to me, darling."

Chapter Eight

I fled, pursued down streets slick with freezing rain, luminous beneath the streetlights overhead. I tripped and fell, scraping my knees on broken glass. I struggled to my feet and continued on. I rushed toward the familiar buildings of the university.

"Nana, help me!"

Where was her voice coming from? Ahead, the street was deserted.

"Nana!"

I saw her face in my mind, anguished in pain and fear.

"I'm here, Mila."

I spun around desperately trying to locate the sound of her voice. I reached the courtyard between the Economics and Physical Sciences buildings.

Under the spotlights, shrouded in mist, I saw two men dressed in full fencing gear, faces covered, engaging in a violent battle. Their attack and parry were interspersed with grunts and raucous laughter that belied the friendly competition.

"My point!"

"I'm still ahead," said the other man, regaining his balance. Laughing, he sprang up and thrust his sabre toward his opponent's shoulder.

"Max! Deszo! Where is Mila? Didn't you hear her cries for help?" I rushed toward my husband, reaching out for his arm. At the same instant, Deszo leapt up, and moved his sabre toward me with the full force of his weight.

A searing pain ripped through my chest, knocking me backward. I coughed and knew my lungs were filling, drowning me with my own blood. I touched my lips, and the warm liquid oozed over my hands. I tumbled down a tunnel surrounded by hideous screams.

Chapter Nine

Choking, I sat up in bed, bathed in sweat, and my heart pounding in my chest.

I heard a crash, and then swearing. I shook off the shock of the nightmare and fixed on the threat within my home.

Silently, I lifted my feet from under the comforter and placed them on the cold floor. I slipped toward the door. Slowly, I retraced my route. I needed a weapon. I scanned the room and then walked toward the closet.

My foot stumbled on a slipper, twisting my ankle. I stifled a cry of pain. I managed to reach the closet door and open it. My lungs filled with the sweet, painful scent of Max as I pushed his old suits aside.

My fingertips felt the cold, steel blade as I

reached up to grab the handle of the old sabre. I heard Max chuckle. During the early days of our marriage, I'd ridiculed his pursuit of this traditional, Hungarian sport. He replied that a genuine Russian could handle any weapon with ease.

Pulling the sabre from the closet, I weighed it in my hand. It was heavier than I'd imagined, as its dull-edged blade was made for fencing, not slicing—but it would help.

I retraced my steps across the room and into the hall. Books fell against what I knew to be the empty shelves that had held my china. The other bedroom doors were closed. I hoped Anna had taken her customary sleeping pill. Mila was another matter.

I hurried to my study, threw on the light, and stepped into the room.

"You came back for the china?" I asked.

Regaining his composure, he smiled and bent to pick up the sack without taking his eyes off the sabre I held pointed towards his chest. "Yes."

I surveyed the empty shelves. "At least you

have good taste."

He looked now from the sabre to my face. He paused and then explained, "I didn't know who would be chosen."

"But when you went to the station this morning and saw Bela and Ilona, you figured it out. Two women and a young girl were left behind," I suggested. "No great threat."

"You should have remained in your room."

"You've done enough harm." I raised the sabre to the height of his chest.

He slung the bag over his shoulder. "You think you can stop me with that?"

My hand shook, but I held firm. "I will."

"Nana?"

His eyes went to the door.

I called out, "Mila, go back to bed."

"No."

I saw the knife in her hand.

Mila's voice carried a quiet authority. "Put the bag down and leave."

He smirked, but there was enough uncertainty to know he was playing at bravado. I stepped toward him. "What's your name?"

"Jozef." He didn't take his eyes from Mila.

I needed to change the atmosphere, to de-escalate the confrontation. "Jozef, my name is Natalie. This is my niece, Mila."

"Of course," he said. "Let me go."

"Nana, what're you doing?"

"He's the ticket seller," I explained.

"You," she hissed. "You tricked my mother!"

"No," Jozef said.

"There were supposed to be five tickets."

I held out my arm to interrupt her. "Mila, you don't understand."

"Your mother knew there were only two tickets," he said.

"No!" Mila ran forward, her knife thrust toward Jozef. "No! You are lying!"

He grabbed her wrist, pulling her into his chest. She screamed as he twisted the knife from her hand and it clattered to the ground.

Throwing Mila to one side, Jozef stooped to pick up the knife. Mila thrust her foot in front of his hand and kicked the knife over to me.

Jozef lunged across the floor as I knelt for the weapon, and Mila jumped onto his back just as he grabbed the knife.

I watched in horror as they rolled away from me, Mila's fist pounding against him. With a jerk, he threw her onto her back, pinned her arms beneath his knees, and put the knife to her throat.

"NO!"

Jozef pressed the knife to Mila's flesh. "Drop the sabre and hand me the bag."

"Don't Nana," Mila's voice was hoarse. "He'll kill us both."

The memory of Deszo and Max fencing flashed before me. I heard Deszo's voice laughing as he parried Max's attack, "You Russian fool! Technique always wins over brute force."

I lifted the sabre as if to hand it to him, then swiveling the blade I brought it down slashing into his arm. The edge of the sabre was too dull to tear his clothing, but the strength of the blow knocked the knife from his hand and he cried out in pain.

Again, they scrambled for the knife.

"Enough!" I screamed. "Stop this madness."

Mila reached the blade first and rolled onto her back. She scuttled across the floor using her legs like a crab. She stopped with her back propped up against the bookcase, holding the knife in both her hands, she gasped, "You bastard, I'll kill you."

"You don't have the strength," Jozef laughed.

I stepped between the two. "I said, that's enough! No one wins here."

Jozef leaned back on his arms, panting as he regarded me from the floor. In an instant, I realized we no longer faced any threat from him. There was something in his eyes, caution, not aggression. He fancied himself a businessman, not a crook. He was as desperate as we were, but for different reasons. Where we saw danger, he saw the opportunity to make a profit. Max once told me that when you understand a man's motive, you know how to deal with him.

"We still need to find a way to safety," I said. "At least for Mila."

He gazed at Mila and smiled sadly. "The Nazis are here," he said looking over his shoulder as if expecting to see them enter the room at their mention. My eyes followed, expecting the same. "If they don't get you, our own Arrow Cross soldiers will."

I shuddered recalling the force of their brutality. I was no longer sure which enemy was worse, the Germans or our own countrymen. "You could get us more tickets," I said. "At least one."

"There are no more trains out."

"Is there any other way you can help us?" I bargained. "I have money."

He rose to his feet, dusting off his pants, then leaned over and grasped the sack. "So do I."

I moved closer and tapped his back with the sabre. "You won't leave with that."

"What will you do?" He scoffed.

"We don't need to repeat our fight." I measured the sabre in my hand.

His eyes again went to Mila. She straightened, and held the knife against her side, regarding him. Her hair had come loose from its braid, and now lay in loose ringlets across her shoulders. Her face, reddened from the exertion of the fight, made her look as if she were wearing rouge and lipstick. I imagined that Jozef was gradually recognizing her beauty.

"I can help you in other ways," he offered.

"How," I asked.

He shook his head and chuckled, "I need money."

"You've got money, from the tickets!" Mila said.

He lifted the bag onto his shoulder. "That money won't last long, prices are rising."

"You said you could help us. How?"

He shrugged his shoulders. "I know of safe houses where they are hiding Jews."

I'd heard similar rumors, but had no idea if they were true. I'd also heard of Jews having been promised safety, only to never be heard from again. "How?"

"I do business with them," he smiled. "For a price, I get them supplies, documents…things."

Mila scoffed, "And we should trust *you*?"

"You have no choice." He smiled. His dark eyes startling in their cunning and also, I realized, in their magnetism. "You trusted me to get the tickets."

"And you cheated us!"

"Not me," he said, and then his smile faded. "The two who got on that train cheated you."

"Put down the bag, and let's talk." I motioned him to the chair where I sat last night. "I'll make coffee."

Jozef regarded me for a long moment and then Mila. He started to say something and then stopped. He shrugged, sighed, carried the bag of my belongings to the chair, and sat down. "I'm hungry."

Mila snapped, "We're not going to share what little food we have with you!"

"I'll find something," I said.

Mila followed me across the room and seethed, "Nana, this boy was trying to rob us, and now you offer him coffee?"

"He may be able to help us," I said. "That he was trying to steal from us is not surprising. I'm only glad he didn't kill us first."

"I don't trust him," she said.

"Neither do I," I replied. "But that has nothing

to do with his ability to help us."

Turning from Mila, I carried a cup of coffee across the room to our guest. It was a gesture of hope.

Chapter Ten

I woke to the sound of someone pounding on the front door. I scrambled out of bed and found Mila standing in the hallway, staring at the door.

"Should I answer it?" She whispered.

"No, go to my room and close the door." I pushed her down the hall and hurried to the front door. "Who is it?"

"It's David, from the university."

"What do you want?" I asked through the closed door.

"It's about your sister."

"She no longer works there," I said my heart pounding.

"I know, but she's there now!" he yelled back.

"She can't be, she's here," I yelled. "Anna! Anna come here!"

There was no response to my call.

I hurried down the hall to her room. Opening her door, I found the room empty, the bed covers tossed aside and her closet door open. The robe and pajamas she wore last night lay in a jumbled pile on the floor.

My heart filled with panic. I fled down the hall, opening and slamming doors, looking in the bathroom, my study, the dining room, and the kitchen, calling her name. There was no answer.

I went to Mila's room and found her sitting up in bed. We'd spent most of the night negotiating with Jozef and finally he'd left before the dawn's first light, promising to return in a few days with more information. Afterwards, Mila and I had gone to our respective bedrooms to sleep for a few hours. "Have you seen Anna this morning?"

Her eyes were wide with fright. "I've only been awake for a little while. I haven't heard anything."

I ran to the front door and flung it open. "Where's my sister?"

The young student standing before me

flinched and then straightening up, confused. "But I thought you were, I mean, I..."

"We're twins," I replied recognizing his confusion. "Now where is she?"

"Oh," he recovered and then explained. "She's at the university."

"What's she doing there?"

He shrugged, his cheeks flushed in embarrassment. "Giving a lecture."

"That's not possible!" I said. "Who are you? And who sent you on this terrible practical joke?"

He squared his shoulders and his cheeks colored with a crimson blush. "It's not a joke. I was one of her students before she left. I'm a poet!"

"Are you sure she was there?" I asked. "This morning?"

"She's not here, is she?" He snapped. "Look we don't have time. She refuses to understand that she's no longer a professor. She's giving a lecture, they're afraid of what she'll say. The Dean sent me to find you. Before the police arrive."

"Oh my God," I gasped. "Wait a moment while I change." I rushed to my room and found

Mila sitting on the edge of my bed. I quickly explained the situation.

She got up and hurried to the door. "I'm coming with you."

"You can't," I said, grabbing for the dress I'd discarded last night. "It's too dangerous."

"You'll need my help!"

"Mila, I've told everyone that you left with your mother, you can't be seen."

"But I can't stay here."

"For now, you must." I sat on the edge of the bed and struggled into my stockings and shoes. "I don't have time to argue."

I got up and met Mila at the door. Embracing her, I whispered in her ear, "Please, I know it's hard, but please—stay here."

She didn't respond, but met my gaze with sad, frustrated eyes that reminded me she was still a young girl.

I met David at the front door, and we hurried down the stairs together and out into the street toward the university.

~*~

The long hall of the university's tiled floor echoed with the clatter of our heels. We ran by classrooms that had emptied to follow the crowd down the hall. Although the location of her former classroom was familiar to me, the throng of students and professors outside the doorway was a sure indication that we'd reached our destination.

I couldn't see Anna over the heads of the students in front of me, but I could hear her voice. Her words were indistinct. Pushing my way through the crowd, I stopped at the doorway and stared.

Standing at the front of the room, behind the podium, was my sister. Thankfully, she'd exchanged her ball gown for an old green tweed suit she frequently wore to lectures. Her wild blonde hair was neatly pulled back in a bun at the nape of her neck. Her face was pale, but radiant.

Her composure astonished me. Her shoulders were back, and her head held high, commanding her audience. Gone was the wild, lost look in her eyes and before me stood a woman I'd rarely seen in the past year. In shock, I couldn't move, couldn't breathe. The students sat in rapt attention. The room was silent, except for her voice. I watched in awe as she paced behind the table, her hands clasped behind her back, warming to her subject.

"War seems to be the way of the world. In history books, we read of military campaigns led by men with maps, armies marked by pushpins, their progress shown by arrows drawn in ink. These Generals plan their assault safely tucked in bunkers of reinforced concrete. Who are we to them? We are nameless, faceless ants."

There was a murmur in the crowd. From one corner of the room, a young man raised his first and yelled his agreement.

She shook her head and laughed. "Merely bugs. Ordered about, stepped upon. Destroyed at will!"

No, Anna—I gasped. *Please no.* I recalled the look in her eyes last night. I saw it again before me now. "No, not here!" I whispered.

Her brows furrowed in anger. "The problem

with this perspective is that it sanitizes the event. They see an aerial view of a city.

"Well, imagine that camera drops down through the clouds to a street amongst the buildings and into a window, and there, it captures the events of a single family. Mothers standing before dinner tables where there is no more food!"

"Fathers and sons shipped off to battlefields or labor camps where they are never heard from again. Children gunned-down in streets where they used to play. That is where you will see the real impact of this war."

"On the streets," yelled a young girl with braids wrapped around her head. "Where they are killing us!"

Another student stood and screamed, "The Fascists! Hitler's accomplices are turning against their own countrymen!"

The students yelled their approval.

The hairs on the back of my neck stood, and I waved my arm to try to attract my sister's attention. I couldn't let her go on. The crowd pushed me backwards, and I struggled to stay on my feet. The walls of the room closed around me, and the temperature rose with the crush of students.

The wound on my head ached, and I felt dizzy. I grasped the shoulder of the man in front of me, afraid I would faint. He turned and smiled as if I were a comrade in this charade.

Anna raised her voice to shout over the rising chorus. "Yes! There, beneath the slogans of dictators shouted over loudspeakers, in between the air-raid sirens, and runs to the basement to hide, the sun continues to rise and set. Food must be found, sleep must be had, and just one more day survived..."

The applause began. Anna shouted over the noise, "While we wonder when the nightmare will end!"

A group in the last row began a chant of "When, when, when, when..."

Didn't she realize what she was doing? In her efforts to speak against what had happened to me on the street, she was putting us in greater danger. Anna's eyes sparkled as she looked around the room. Her voice rose as she raised her arms into the air.

"It is our responsibility as artists to raise our voices against the war. We must wage a battle with words."

The crowd roared their approval. I shuddered, and yelled for her to stop.

"We must speak out against the soldiers who would kill us. We must use our pens as swords against the hate that sends our loved ones away from us!"

A young man standing near me at the door, raised his fist and yelled, "Communists! Traitors!" He shoved against me, and I ducked as a scuffle began.

Anna's bright-red cheeks radiated the passion behind her words. "We will not hide from the enemy. We will not be silent! We will tell them that we have had enough of their guns and tanks and bombs!"

The crowd exploded in a chorus. "Yes!"

"To the streets!"

"Down with the Fascists!"

I failed to reach my sister, as students rushed toward her and simultaneously began shouting-down dissenters. All around the room, arguments and scuffles broke out.

I clawed my way through the hordes, screaming, "Anna! Anna!"

She turned toward my voice and then moved away to the other side of the room.

"Anna! Stop!"

My cries were lost in the melee.

Behind me, the crowd surged, and I toppled against the rows of desks in front of me. I flung myself into the crowd that moved in the irrational ebb and flow of a tide simultaneously trying to move in and out of the room.

"Anna!" I could see her still at the front of the room. As students pressed against her, she became disoriented. Horrified, I watched her face transform as her mind opened and she slipped through a door that led her away. I heard a young woman scream, and the crowd surged backwards as someone yelled that the police had arrived.

I heard them before I saw them. Their shouts

filled the air, followed by a chorus of screams and curses from the students they beat with their clubs. The air around me was thick with the movement of bodies flung in disarray. Panic turned the tide from exaltation to self-preservation.

Unfortunately, there was only one exit. A doorway filled by the enemy. Many of the triumphant quickly became lambs, grabbing their books, cowering and bowing their heads in silence. A few, brave souls continued to rage. They raged as they ducked.

Then there was Anna. My darling sister. Swimming against the tide, she stood and laughed. She continued to laugh as the police surrounded her. She laughed as they grabbed her arms and yanked her away from the podium.

"Stay…" she laughed hysterically, breaking free one last time, she raised her arms above her head as if conducting her orchestra.

"Stay!" She screamed as they surrounded her and lifted her by her arms and dragged her from the room.

I followed the police escort into the hall. "Wait,

I'm her sister!"

They ignored my pleas. My attempts to get Anna's attention failed in her reverie.

With no other recourse, I followed the police down the hall to the Dean's office.

Despite my protests, I was not allowed in the room. What would happen to her now? Would they arrest her and put her in jail? Would she be carted off to one of the labor camps? Or worse, to an asylum?

Someone put a hand on my shoulder, and I whirled around to see the Dean of the university. "You've got to help me," I grabbed his sleeve. "Anna's in trouble."

"What was she thinking? She's caused a great deal of trouble."

"Can you get me in there? I can explain her illness to them. She didn't know what she was saying."

"I'm not sure they'll believe you."

"They have to!"

"Let me go in first and intervene." He squeezed my arm and then left me. When the door opened, I couldn't see Anna over the coats of the policemen. I cried out for her, but my voice was lost as the door shut in my face.

I turned and hurried down the hall and up the stairs to the second floor. Glass-fronted doors leading to the individual offices of the faculty divided the wood-paneled hall.

At the end of the hall, there was a cul-de-sac of three offices. I knocked on the one to my left. My knock was answered by a voice issuing an invitation to enter. With trembling hands, I turned the knob and opened the door.

The overhead light shadowed his face as he sat bent over his desk. When I entered the room, he glanced up, sighed, and then returned to the book he was studying.

He appeared the same as I'd remembered, though as I stepped into the room, it became clear that creases above his brow and around his eyes softened his chiseled features. Sprinklings of silver frosted his dark hair.

"It's me, Natalie. Not Anna," I said, stopping before his desk.

He leaned back in his chair, and his frown became a hesitant smile. "I know. It's been a long time."

I kept in mind that they had not broken up easily. Anna had fought his rationalization that the affair had come to its natural end with painful, sometimes hysterical, entreaties that had led to embarrassing arguments in front of the other faculty. I often wondered if their breakup had precipitated Anna's descent into her imaginary world, or whether his recognition of her decline caused him to seek an end, rather than watch her fall.

"Deszo, I need your help."

"It's good to see you, Natalie."

His voice. I'd forgotten the effect his smooth, masculine voice had on me. I shook off the start of a memory. "I'm sorry, I don't have time to be polite. Anna's in trouble."

"I don't think I'm the right person for you to see."

I placed my hands on his desk. "Deszo, please, they're holding her downstairs in the Dean's office."

"What's she doing here?"

"Please, come now," I said reaching for his hand. "I'll explain it as we go."

"I don't want to get involved..."

"Deszo, she came here believing she was still a professor. She gave an inflammatory speech. They've called the police!"

"But..."

My fists pounded the desk. "Damn it, this has nothing to do with your affair. I'm asking you as a friend."

"Whose friend?"

"For Max."

Deszo's eyebrows arched, and he looked at me without comment.

"Then do it for me."

He stood and walked around his desk. I grabbed his arm in mine and hurried him down the hall. As we moved down the stairs, I explained my confrontation with the soldiers last night, the event that I believed had precipitated her actions this morning. Deszo stopped on the landing under the light from a window and touched my forehead. "Natalie."

"We don't have time." I said, brushing his hand away. "Please, hurry."

The crowd around the Dean's office had subsided when we reached the door. A policeman answered Deszo's knock. We explained our relationship to Anna, and the officer stepped aside. Deszo went in first, and I followed behind him.

"Where's Anna?"

The Dean nodded towards his office. "I had them put her in there. I felt it would be less stressful for her."

"Thank you," I said, heading for the door.

I entered the room quietly. My heart skipped when I found the room empty. Then I heard the chair behind the desk squeak on its castors, and it rolled a little closer to the window.

Walking over to the chair, I saw Anna. Her palm, pressed against the cold glass left a moist impression.

As I reached for her, she spoke, leaving my hand in mid-air.

"It's colder than usual this winter."

I nodded and looked at the barren trees in the courtyard outside the window. "Yes."

"I was looking for birds."

"Anna, don't."

"There aren't any people in the park to feed them." Her voice took on a singsong quality. "To throw breadcrumbs on the sidewalk for them."

"People are starving, Anna."

"But who will feed the birds?" She whispered in a childlike tone.

"I don't know," I said.

"They'll die if someone doesn't feed them."

"Is that why you are here?"

She shrugged, but refused to turn away from the window. "Do you remember when we were little, how Marie would let us put breadcrumbs on the windowsill in the kitchen?"

"Yes," I said, wondering how Anna's demeanor had so drastically changed. Her hair had come loose from the neat bun at the nape of her neck, releasing wisps of blonde curls. She swayed in her seat, keeping rhythm to a song I couldn't hear. Her voice slipped between the ebullient confidence I'd heard only an hour before, and the childish banter of her dementia, as if the two warred within her for authority.

"And when we came home from school in the afternoon, we would go to the window and see that all the breadcrumbs were gone. Marie said that the birds had come while we were at school."

I smiled and touched the collar of her jacket, letting my fingers run along the nubby tweed, wishing I could join her in this innocent reflection.

Anna continued without me, "So one Saturday I put out the breadcrumbs as we did every morning. This time, I sat by the window and waited for the birds. But they never came."

Anna's voice broke. "When I asked Marie why they wouldn't come, she just laughed and said, 'Faith is the evidence of things not seen.'"

"I don't understand your point, Anna."

"It's a crazy verse, isn't it?"

"No, not that."

Her voice changed again, taking on the solemn authority I'd heard in the classroom. "I've thought about it a great deal—*The evidence of things not seen.* It contains an inherent contradiction, doesn't it? How can there be evidence of things not seen?"

The steel-gray sky, pregnant with unreleased snow, reflected the desperate frustration of my sister. But I felt no sympathy. "It's describing the mystery of faith."

"I think it describes how difficult it is to believe in God's presence even when we can't see Him, even when we feel so alone and need His presence."

I sighed, exasperated. Wasn't it enough to save Mila? "Anna, some birds will live, and some will die. We cannot save them all."

Anna shook her head and then pressed her forehead against the glass. "If not us, then who will save them?"

"Is that why you came here?" I repeated.

"Someone has to feed the birds," she whispered. "If not us, then who, Natalie? Will God save them? Or are we meant to be His helpers?"

There was a knock on the door. Deszo entered. He stopped when Anna turned around as if not sure of her reaction to seeing him.

Anna merely blinked and then smiled. "Hello, darling! Have you come to take me to dinner?"

To my surprise, Deszo smiled and said, "Yes, I have."

Anna swept from the chair into Deszo's arms. As he held her, he looked over her shoulder at me and smiled sadly. Releasing her, he held her at arm's length and said, "Since Natalie is here, it would be rude if we didn't invite her along."

"Of course." Anna glanced back at me with a jubilant smile. "Natalie, call Max and ask him if he can join us."

I coughed and shook my head. "Max isn't available. It will just have to be the three of us."

I approached Deszo with a questioning look, "Is everything settled now?"

He nodded toward Anna who had gone back to the desk to gather her coat. "Actually, her salvation was a matter of politics. Since she was neither Jewish nor a Communist, they quickly lost interest. Good for her, too bad for the students who were."

"We're lucky you were here," I said.

Deszo smiled bitterly, "You won't be so lucky next time, Natalie. The Arrow Cross will be ruthless now that the Germans have arrived. They're not only rounding up the Jews, but anyone else who tries to speak out against their plans."

When we entered the outer office, the police were gone. The Dean stood in the center of the room nervously stroking his beard.

"Thank you," I said, grasping his hand. "Thank you for your help."

He nodded to where Anna stood wrapping her scarf around her neck, humming a melody as she tucked the ends into her coat. "Natalie, your sister was a great poet."

"Is," I countered.

"No, not anymore," he said, shaking his head. "In different times, her outburst would have been regarded as the eccentricity of a brilliant but wounded mind. But now, she is a danger."

"I know," I nodded sadly.

"Not just to herself. But to others, to the university. I won't defend her next time."

I looked into his eyes, but he turned his head, releasing my grip on his hand. "She's no longer welcome here." He walked to his office and closed the door.

Chapter Eleven

When we left the building, I was surprised to see that it had started to snow. The walkway that bisected the park leading to the street was dusted with white, muffling the sounds of the city.

Bare tree branches caught snowflakes in their outstretched arms and slowed their descent to earth. I felt cut off from the rest of the world, safe in this winter landscape. The scene could have been any one of many happy memories of the three of us leaving the university to meet Max for dinner.

How many evenings had Anna and I walked on either side of Deszo, our arms linked through his, laughing at the double-takes we'd get as people stared, from me to Anna, noticing our identical faces, and the proud way Deszo escorted us as if we both belonged to him.

I suppose, in some way, he actually believed that. Max would meet us outside the restaurant, and I'd break from Deszo's grip to rush over and kiss my true love. We'd tuck into a table and spend the next three hours drinking wine and sharing the day's events. At the end of the meal, Deszo would light a cigarette, Max his pipe, and Anna and I would lean toward one another and begin to whisper.

Then the evening would continue at a café for coffee and dessert. How happy we'd all been. Our lives were successful and our futures bright. In this moment, I wanted to trade places with Anna, to stay in the window to the past, as I am longing for all that was now gone.

Deszo and I walked on either side of Anna, each of us holding her elbows. Anna chattered happily, leaning her head back to catch snowflakes on her face. I followed her upward gaze and then turned to look back at the window where she'd sat with her hand pressed against the glass like a child.

At the edge of the park, we saw the crowd waiting for the tram. We joined them, stamping our feet against the cold that seeped through the soles of our leather shoes. We stood with our backs to the biting wind. Fifteen minutes later, it was clear that the tram had stopped running or would be impossibly full by the time it reached us.

"I need to get home to Mila," I said to Deszo.

"Isn't Ilona there with her?"

"No, she left with Bela, yesterday."

Deszo looked startled then angry. "She left Mila."

"Yes," I said.

"Why?"

"I don't know." I brushed the snow from Anna's shoulders and pulled her collar closed around her scarf. "But she's my responsibility now. I have to get home."

"We'll have to walk," he said. We started down the sidewalk, Anna still between us, oblivious to her surroundings. At the corner, we turned up a side street, and saw a commotion of blaring horns and blocked traffic. In the middle of the street, a delivery truck had apparently broken down and was blocking the cars behind it.

As we passed the truck, we saw a German soldier standing on the running board of a military car bearing Nazi flags. He waved a gun, and was screaming at the driver of the truck. Suddenly the German fired his gun into the air, and I struggled to hold onto Anna as she shrieked and pulled from my grasp.

Screams pierced the air as the blast from the gun amplified and echoed against the walls. All around us, people fell to the ground or ran, taking cover in doorways. Next to me, a child cried out as her mother grabbed her hand and pulled her into a store.

The German, encouraged by the mayhem, shouted, "Run, rabbits!" as he shot off round after round from his pistol. Ducking, I pushed Anna over the bodies that lay in our path.

"Are you crazy? Where are you going?" Deszo grabbed me and shoved us against a wall, covering us with his body.

"We have to get out of here."

The sulphur smoke of gunfire mixed with the exhaust fumes from the stalled traffic created a stifling cloud between the apartment buildings that crouched on either side of the narrow street. Beneath me, Anna moaned, and I moved to take the weight off her arm.

I glanced over my shoulder and watched the German stop abruptly as a senior officer got out of the car and started yelling at him. The first soldier saluted and then, holstering his gun, walked over to the driver of the truck. Yelling and gesturing toward a couple of men on the sidewalk, he orchestrated the truck to move onto the sidewalk on the other side of the street.

Brushing his soiled hands down the length of his coat, the German swore as he got into the car and slammed the door. In a moment, his car had disappeared down the street.

"Is this what we can expect from the occupation?" I asked Deszo, as I helped Anna to her feet.

Deszo held his left shoulder with his right hand, slowly rotating it while looking across the street to the abandoned truck. "This was a mere pleasantry. They know they are losing the war, so they are desperate. Be glad you're not a Jew."

Anna stepped over to Deszo, began massaging his shoulder, and said the words that I had been thinking. "Mila is a Jew. What will happen to her?"

Deszo shrugged off Anna's hand and then linked his arms in both of ours. He steered us up the street, and we made our way home without further conversation.

Mila opened the front door to our apartment as soon as I put the key into the lock. She was surprised to see Deszo, but took his coat without question. I told Deszo to wait for me in my study, and I followed Anna down the hall telling her to wash up. Mila was standing in the hall when I left Anna's room. She followed me into the kitchen and sat at the table while I began to prepare our dinner.

"Why were you gone so long? What happened?" Taking the small knife and potato from my shaking hands, she began quickly peeling the skin onto the tabletop. She kept her head bowed, but with a swipe of her arm, wiped a tear onto her sleeve. "I was afraid you weren't coming back."

"Mila, I'm sorry I had to leave you alone. I had to go to Anna. She was in a great deal of trouble."

Mila made no reply, but shook off my hands and took up her task with the potato. I clasped my hands together and watched her butcher one potato after another as the tears streamed down her face. I felt helpless beneath her silent recrimination. Abandoned not once, but twice, in two days. I couldn't help it. I had to help my sister. She was all I had left of my family.

I realized that, in the flurry of events, I had not found a moment to sit with Mila and explain why her mother had left her at the train station. Did she feel betrayed by me, as well? I reached for Mila, wanting to pull her to my chest. As my hands reached her shoulders, she jerked away as if scalded by my touch. Her face filled with anger, her jaw taut with unspoken accusations.

Then her hands stopped. "They were here."

"Who?" My heart tightened.

"The Nazis."

"Here? In this apartment?"

"In the building." She stood up, walked to the

counter, and retrieved a piece of paper. "They knocked on the door, but I didn't answer. Then they shoved it under the door and said that they would be back."

I took the piece of paper from her hands, my eyes skimmed down the page before I was able to make sense of the words. It was a notice requiring all Jews to report to the local police precinct for registration.

"But why would they come here? The apartment is registered in my family's name."

"Miss Szep said they slid one under every door in the building."

Miss Szep was an elderly spinster who lived alone, below us. She rarely came out of her apartment, except to complain about Bela's drunken tirades. "When did you speak with her?"

"After the Nazis left, she came to the door. She said that she was alone."

"Still, I wish you wouldn't have answered the door. No one should know that you are here."

"She saw Bela and Mom leave without us yesterday and then when she saw us return without them, she said she figured out why."

Miss Szep dedicated several hours of each day to watching the street below, and was therefore aware of the comings and goings of everyone in the building, all from her front window.

At times, the only reminder that any one lived in her apartment was the flutter of a curtain if you happened to look up as you approached the building from the street. Most of the time there was little sign of her, with the exception of the smell of delicious poppy seed rolls baking in her oven, the product sometimes ending up as an anonymous gift propped against our front door.

"Still, she knows that you're here," I said. "What if they question her?"

"She said she would tell the truth," Mila said.

I gasped. "No!"

"She will tell the soldiers she saw me leave with my parents. That the only people living in this apartment are two sisters, both good Catholics."

I leaned back in my chair and stared at the ceiling. Miss Szep was at least eighty. She'd known my parents, my husband, and before the arrival of

Bela and Ilona, she'd been a frequent guest in our home. Could she be trusted? Who else had seen Mila return with us? I thought of Mrs. Nyugati. There were too many like her, people who wouldn't hesitate to give Mila away if it meant gaining their own advantage with the enemy.

Chapter Twelve

Mila looked up, and I turned to see Deszo standing in the doorway. "Have I interrupted?"

"No, sit down," I smiled. "I'm sorry I left you alone in the study. Anna must have decided to take a bath."

"Actually, she's in the study reading." He took a seat across from me. "She seems to think we've spent the day together, which I suppose is correct in a way. Anyway, she's reading a book of her poems. I hope not preparing for another lecture."

"God, no," I sighed. "I'll have to explain the situation to her again. And then keep an eye on her."

Mila shot me a questioning look for an explanation. I raised my eyebrows and rolled my eyes.

Deszo chuckled. "You know if it hadn't been so dangerous, it would have been funny."

"If she'd confined her lecture to poetry instead of politics, yes." I took up Mila's task of peeling the potatoes.

"So what are we going to do about you?" Deszo nodded toward Mila.

"I'm going to stay here."

"I don't think it's safe," Deszo said.

I quickly told Deszo of Mila's experience with the Germans and showed him the notice. Then I told him about Jozef and the safe houses.

Deszo held the notice in his hands, shaking his head. "They're moving more quickly than I'd imagined. This Jozef is right about the safe houses, though I'm not sure I would trust someone who had tried to rob your house. The Swedish and Swiss consulates are issuing documents for safe passage in an effort to bring the Jews under their protection."

"I want Mila here with us," I said. "I'd feel better knowing she was with us instead of strangers."

"But in doing so, you may be endangering her as well as yourself and Anna," he countered.

"Nana, you can't do that." Mila reached for my hand, and I put down my work to give her a brief squeeze.

"What can we do?" I looked at Deszo, but he didn't lift his attention from the page. "After all, how much longer can the war go on? The Allies are coming, and I've heard that the Russians are close to our border. Surely, the Germans can't be bothered with rounding up Jews now."

Deszo held out the notice. "What further proof do you need?"

I pushed the paper away and got up from the table. "I can't believe this. What will they do? Register the Jews and then what? Send them home?"

I picked up the potatoes, carried them over to the stove, and dropped them into a pot of water. I took out a frying pan and began cutting the kielbasa into rough chunks, letting them fall into the pan. "Mila, please go set the table for dinner."

I waited until she'd left the room before

turning to Deszo. "Are the rumors true? Will they send them to labor camps, as they did in Poland?"

"Natalie, they don't come back from those labor camps."

"No, it can't be. I've heard people say that they've gotten letters from families sent there."

"Those are false rumors, spread by the Germans," he said. "They're not true."

I wiped my hands on a towel and looked around the room for something, I couldn't remember what. I felt helpless and overwhelmed.

"I have some contacts through the university," he continued. "People sympathetic to helping the work of the consulates. Let me speak with them. I'll contact you tomorrow. In the meantime, do not let Mila leave the apartment. She should not register. Tell anyone who asks that she has left with her parents."

~*~

We ate together in the dining room. Mila had set the table with white linen and candles. Anna came to the table wearing a simple gray wool dress, her hair once again pulled back into a neat bun.

Deszo sat at the head of the table with Anna on one side of him and Mila on the other. In spite of all that had happened today, they had a lively conversation, Deszo asking Mila about her studies, Anna about her poetry. It was clear that he had decided not to dwell on the realities we faced. At least not during our meal together. I picked at my food and idly glanced out the window at the last flurries of snow.

"I feel inspired," Anna said picking up her glass of wine. "I'd like to make a toast, to my return to the university and to Deszo's return to my life."

"I'll make coffee," I said.

"Let's have it in your study, in front of the stove," Deszo suggested.

I nodded and cleared the plates from the table. Mila offered to help, but I shook my head. "Perhaps you could interest Deszo in a game of backgammon."

I piled the dishes in the sink and put the kettle on to boil. I went to the window next to the stove and peered down to the alleyway. The snow had stopped, and where it had fallen there were puddles of ugly, black slush.

In a strange way, I was glad the beauty I'd witnessed in the park was gone. The Germans didn't deserve to see our city in its winter splendor. They deserved what they brought with them, filth, coldness, and despair.

My fingertips brushed against the windowpane. Yes, I recalled feeding the birds when we were young. I remembered the verse our housekeeper had quoted. It was about faith— the hope in the unseen. It was *my* memory, not hers. I am the bird feeder. I was the one who sat by the window that day and waited for the birds that never came, not Anna.

I went back to the sink and picked up a crust of bread from one of the plates. Tearing it into tiny pieces, I remembered that two days ago, March Nineteenth, was the day the Germans had finally come, and it was a Sunday. I hadn't gone to Mass. I hadn't even thought of it.

Now as I rolled the bits of bread into tiny balls,

I was hungry for Communion, for evidence of God's presence. Then I thought of Anna's question in the Dean's office. Were we meant to be God's helpers now?

Was that part of faith? Showing the willingness to step into the unknown and simply believe that God would be there with us? Would I be asked to do that for Mila? Or for Anna? Would I be able to take that step into thin air and believe that God will be with me no matter what?

A sliver of cold air sliced the warmth of the kitchen when I opened the window. Opening my hand, I laid the crumbs in a careful row on the ledge. Then I closed the window, went to the stove and took the kettle into the study to join the others.

mrs. tuesday's departure

Chapter Thirteen

In the corner of the study, Mila dozed, curled in the arms of a green velvet wingback chair. It was well after midnight. I stifled a yawn, ignoring the resistance of my stiff joints as I pushed myself from my chair. A disappointed cry from an interrupted dream escaped Mila's lips as I roused her from her sleep and guided her out of the study. She stopped in front of the doors leading to the living room.

"I want to see their room," she said, leaving my side and entering the room.

She turned on a lamp, illuminating the room that had been converted into a bedroom for Ilona and Bela. The bed covers were tossed on the floor, and clothes were scattered around the room as evidence they had packed in a hurry.

Mila walked around the room, picking up

items of her mother's clothing, folding them and placing them on the bed.

"Mila you haven't mentioned your mother."

Mila kept her back to me and continued folding the clothes. "I think of her all the time."

I too had thought of Ilona, wondering if she'd safely made it to Switzerland. Wondering if her heart ached because she abandoned her only child. "I can't explain what she did. But I know that she loves you."

Mila cringed at the words. "Nana, were you surprised that she left without me?"

"Of course," I said, although the truth was that I wasn't surprised. I'd hoped, no more than that. I'd prayed that just this once Ilona would put her daughter first.

"I'm not," she said, picking up one of Bela's jackets and then throwing it down. "I don't know why she doesn't like me. I tried to stay out of the way; I tried to be a brilliant student..." Mila turned to me; her features were contorted with hurt and frustration. She held her mother's sweater in her hand and then lifted it to her nose and inhaled deeply. "I miss her, Nana." She dropped the sweater on the bed. "Maybe she will send for me."

Isn't that the greatest tragedy?

When someone rejects us, no matter how they abuse our love, we hope against reason that somehow they will come back to us.

I knew from the look on Ilona's face as the train left the station that she did not intend to ever see her daughter again. But I wouldn't tell that to Mila.

Instead, I walked to Mila and embraced her. "We will find out where she is and then contact her. I'm sure that once she's found a new place to live, maybe when this terrible war is over, I'm sure she'll send for you."

Mila and I left the room, stopping to turn out the light and close the door behind us. We went to her room and, while Mila got ready for bed, I sat in my usual chair and picked up the book of Anna's poetry. The same one Mila had been reading the night before.

Mila turned under the covers and propped herself up on one elbow. "Nana, I must go to a safe house."

"Not yet."

"If the Nazi's find me here, you and Anna will be taken away too."

"Then we'll have to keep you well hidden."

"But what about Anna?"

"I'll speak with her again."

"She can't help herself, Nana."

Anna's insanity was enough to make her dangerous, but not enough to make her harmless. I shivered with guilt at the thought. Would I have to choose between my sister and my niece? I turned off the light, closed Mila's door, and walked down the hall to my study.

Anna was sitting next to Deszo on the sofa, holding his hand, leaning against his shoulder. When I walked in, she looked up at me with half-closed eyes and a smile conveying the satisfaction of a cat. Oddly, Deszo's expression showed acute discomfort his cheeks flushed as he slipped his hand out of Anna's clasp.

"I'm going to bed now," I said. "Deszo, thank you for your help today."

Deszo got up from the couch. "I should go."

"No, stay!" Anna protested. "Natalie leave us."

I turned from them and Deszo followed me to the door.

"Deszo, wait!" Anna hurried to his side, grasping his arm as if to pull him back to the couch. "Spend the night here, with me."

Deszo's cheeks reddened further, and he gently pried her fingers from his arm. "I have to go home now. I'll see you again."

Anna smiled demurely and lifted her face to kiss him on the cheek. "Our next meeting will be more private." She lowered her voice and whispered, while looking at me. "And intimate."

Deszo followed me down the hall to the front door and I helped him into the sleeves of his camelhair coat. The tender caress of its nap contrasted with its weight as it left my hands and lifted over his navy wool jacket. I brushed my fingertips across the seams of the shoulders and shivered with the awareness of his masculine scent.

Deszo turned and clasped his hands to my face. His hooded, blue eyes searched my face and he smiled, sadly. "Natalie, come to my office tomorrow. I'll have more information for you."

I shook my head. "Not the university. Can you come here?"

Deszo glanced down the hall toward the study and frowned. "I can't come here. Anna will believe I'm coming for her." His fingers traveled down my neck and rested on my shoulders.

My cheeks reddened now. "That would be understandable from what I saw."

"Natalie, I want to help you. Not resume a relationship with Anna."

I took a step backwards, out of his grasp. "Max would be grateful for your help."

"Of course." Deszo's smile faded for an instant and then returned. "Meet me at the café across the street from the university. At four o'clock."

He turned and reached for the door. Instinctively, I bowed my body toward it. As he stepped outside, he turned and pulled me into his chest. His arms ran up my back, one hand holding my neck other tilting my head back.

His lips lingered just a moment too long to be a

chaste kiss between old friends. He pressed just a bit too hard.

Gasping, I pulled myself away at the same moment I heard someone else clear their throat in the stairway. I turned and saw an Arrow Cross soldier staring up at us with an embarrassed smile. He was a young boy, seventeen perhaps, with red hair cut close to his scalp. I clutched the edge of the door.

Deszo put his arm around my shoulders pulling me into his side. The squeeze of his fingers silenced me.

"Good evening." The soldier tipped his cap. "Sorry to bother you. We heard there were Jews living in this building and…"

Deszo cut him off with a growl, "I've been wondering when you'd get around to searching here."

The young soldier stiffened. "Sir, we've been making a thorough search of every building, but…"

Deszo released my shoulders and reached into his coat pocket, withdrawing a pen. "What's your name?"

"As you know, Sir, most of our soldiers have been sent to the front. We've been severely understaffed."

"Your name?" Deszo demanded.

The front door slammed downstairs and there was a clamor of footsteps on the stairs. "Elek!"

The young soldier leaned into the stairwell and yelled. "Up here."

"Have you found the Jews?"

Deszo waved him off and yelled down, "You're too late soldier, we had the last lot of Jews shipped out a week ago. And now if you'll follow me, I will show you out to the street so you can introduce me to your commanding officer."

Chapter Fourteen

After Deszo left, I went back to my study and found it empty. My heart was pounding as I walked to Mila's bedroom. The light in her room was off, and as I opened the door, a sliver of light from the hall slid across her bed and outlined her sleeping face. When I opened Anna's door, I saw her sitting at her vanity. She screwed the lid off a jar of cold cream and scooped a dollop into the palm of her hand. She looked at me through the mirror and smiled. "Come in."

"Quite a day," I said, sitting on the edge of her bed. I couldn't decide whether or not to tell her about the soldier's visit. I would not tell her about Deszo's kiss.

Anna began to apply the cream to her face like a thick frosting. "It was a nice surprise to have you show up after my lecture."

I shivered as if feeling the cold cream touching my own face. "Anna, you shouldn't have been there."

Her hand stopped in mid-stroke. "Of course I should!" She picked up a sponge and began to roughly wipe the cold cream off her face. "I have lectures to give."

"No, you don't. You don't work there anymore."

Her eyebrow arched, and she smirked. "Natalie, don't be foolish. I have tenure, they can't fire me!"

I folded my hands in my lap and our eyes met in the mirror's reflection. As Anna tilted her head to the right, I unconsciously did the same. To others, we still appeared identical, but I could see tiny furrows around her eyes and forehead and a slight tick at the corner of her lips.

Her illness had begun to separate us in looks, just as it had in our relationship. It was pointless to argue. On the other hand, I couldn't allow her to instigate a replay of this morning. "Anna, you haven't been a member of the teaching staff at the university in over a year. You were asked to retire."

She leaned toward the mirror and vigorously wiped the remnants of the white cream from her forehead and chin. "Well perhaps I took a sabbatical for a year, but I'm ready to return now. It's clear that I'm still extremely popular with the students."

"You gave an anti-war speech this morning, not a lecture on poetry."

"We are in a war, Natalie." She shook her head. "Really. You accuse *me* of losing my mind. Someone has to speak out."

My cheeks flushed in anger. "Since your memory serves you so well, do you remember that we are hiding Mila? The police will be keeping an eye on you now, which means that they will be watching where you live. Here, where we are trying to hide Mila!"

"Ilona will come back for Mila, won't she?"

"Perhaps, when the war is over," I guessed.

"Natalie, are you surprised that she left Mila behind?"

I turned and checked her bedroom door to make sure that it was closed. "No, I'm not surprised. I'd hoped for a different outcome. Somehow, I believed that if we made it to the train, Ilona would have been shamed into taking Mila."

"How could a mother choose her husband over her own daughter?" Anna's question was rhetorical, but still unanswerable. She shook her head. "Mila must be heartbroken."

"Angry," I replied.

"Ilona not only put Mila in danger, but us as well."

Anna had always treated Ilona with disdain. I believe it began in childhood. Anna always wanted to be our father's princess, the sun around which we all orbited in pale comparison. In school, we competed to see who could get the better grades, Anna always rushing home to show her stellar reports first.

"Look Papa! I scored the highest in the class!"

She would climb into Father's lap, waving her grade card. As she received his kisses, she would look over at me and smile. It was not a pleasant smile. It was triumphant. Father would look up and say, "And what about you, Natalie? Did you come in second?"

My heart sank at those words, but I nodded and held out my card.

"Good! I have the two smartest girls in Budapest!" He would hold out his arms, and I would be embraced in a hug that he meant to be large enough for both of us. My father's love was enormous, enough for twins, for a wife he loved more than his own life, and for a younger daughter. But sometimes, even I wished those arms held only one.

Chapter Fifteen

It was during this time, we were just a few years older than Mila is now, that we began to write. We both started out as poets. My father loved Petofi and Szebo; he claimed poets were the heroes of Hungary. We strived after his admiration by trying to become the best of what he loved. At first, it was innocent fun. We were too young, too dependent upon one another, to allow anything to fully separate us. At night before bed, we gave theatrical performances from our books of poetry and giggled over the love sonnets. We took turns reading our own poetry to our parents. Mother always praised our work. Papa would smile and then give us a commentary on what needed to be improved.

When Ilona showed the least sign of joining

our competition for Father's attention, Anna made fun of her efforts, quashing the young ego as it tried to blossom. She succeeded all too well. Ilona's grades dropped as ours continued to rise. Soon she began skipping school; notes came from her teachers complaining about her absences, her lack of attention, and her preoccupation with boys rather than study. Mother and Father tried to help her, but she took their concern as further evidence of their disappointment in her. Years later, I too would feel the weight of Anna's scorn.

We were at university together. We were both students in the Literature department, both honing our skills as poets. The university sponsored an annual poetry competition. Anna and I entered. We worked for weeks, separately, on a portfolio of poems to submit. Though we shared a room, we each jealously guarded our work, each claiming that we didn't want to influence the other. The truth was that neither one of us wanted to reveal the special work that we felt might be copied.

Our father's face beamed as he told Mother. How he bragged to his colleagues that he had not one, but two daughters in the famous contest. We beamed, because he did.

The weeks we had to endure, waiting for the announcement of the results were torture. We fought more than usual. Our sibling rivalry took an ominous turn toward real spite. Finally, the night arrived.

To underscore the notoriety that came with the grand prize, the university held the ceremony in the National Opera House. Anna and I dressed in black silk gowns, trimmed in inky velvet. Our father, who insisted that we wear matching dresses to show our solidarity, purchased the dresses for us. I put my dress on first. Anna, as she was tonight, sat at the dressing table, doing her make-up.

"Now that the competition is over…" she said as she applied her eyeliner, "tell me what you chose as your theme."

I studied her reflection, and saw my own in the background. I hesitated, "family things."

Her smile faded, and her hand dropped to the table. "Not very sophisticated, is it?" She took up her pencil again. "You know Father believes the great poets are brave enough to speak out about freedom and the future of the nation."

I knew the theme she had chosen. The self-assured smile that returned to her lips provided the evidence and her verdict. She would win, and I would lose. I bit my lip to hide my disappointment. "I'll wait for you in the living room," I said, wanting to leave the room before I gave in to tears.

Anna and I were silent in the car to the opera. Papa joked that we were more nervous than he'd ever seen us. He said this was clearly a sign that we'd both done our best work.

In the theatre, Anna and I sat together, Father sat next to Anna, and Mother next to him. My seat on the end of the row enabled me to watch the contestants make their walk down to the stage where they received their prize. Deszo was also there that evening as my date, though he sat further back.

"And the First Runner Up prize goes to Anna Lucas." The crowd applauded loudly, my father jumped to his feet and beamed. Only I noticed the look of disappointment on my sister's face. When she turned to face our father, her face radiated what I knew was a phony smile. I watched her embrace my father, receive his kisses on her cheeks, and then walk up to the stage to receive her prize.

"The grand prize in poetry goes to," the audience held their breath, "Natalie Lucas for her cycle of poems entitled, "My Father's Smile."

My heart skipped, my father lifted me by the shoulders and kissed me on both cheeks, as he had Anna. I was overcome by the thunderous applause as I made my way toward the stage. As I received my prize, I turned to my sister and saw the rage that filled her eyes.

She leaned over and whispered in my ear, "First you take the man that I love and then you take my prize. I will never forgive you."

But she did in time. I gave up poetry after that contest. And I gave up Deszo.

~*~

Twenty years later, we once again entered into

a battle of wills.

"Anna, you can't go back to the university."

She sighed and turned her back on me. "Natalie, how can we be so different?"

"Anna, do you realize that the Germans have arrived? The Arrow Cross were at our door this evening!"

"Don't be so dramatic." Anna blocked the light from the lamp that sat on the edge of her vanity. As she turned her face from one side to the other, the shadow passed across her face. I shivered reflexively. She leaned back and frowned at her reflection. "I must support the students who are speaking out."

I shot to my feet and grabbed Anna by the shoulders. "And when they come to arrest you, they'll take Mila as well!"

Anna stared at me through the mirror and then tilted her head to one side, resting it against my arm. "She will be better off in one of the safe houses as Deszo suggested."

My grip on her shoulders tightened. "I want her here with me."

"That's selfish."

"You'd rather she go to live with strangers?" I released her shoulders and stared at her reflection in the mirror. "You think Deszo has all the answers."

"Don't be coy, Natalie." Anna's smile turned down at the corners in a smirk. "I noticed the way you were eyeing him tonight. It's shameful actually, with Max only dead a year."

I glared at her and hissed, "Max has been dead for five years, Anna."

A confused look crossed her face and then she quickly regained her composure. Her hands went from one jar to another, tightening down the lids. "How's the book you're working on?"

"The only book that I'm currently working on is the editing of your journals."

"I find inspiration rather than excuses in the war," Anna sniffed. "I've decided to begin a new cycle of poems. But, back to our discussion of Deszo, I hope that you will not use my position at the university to try to see him, as you did today. It's too obvious."

I turned away and paced back toward the bedroom door. I reminded myself again that Anna's dementia skewed her logic. Though it was becoming increasingly difficult to maintain my sympathy. Even in her former years of lucidity, her affair had made her possessive and jealous, ironic since she was the in the position of mistress rather than wife. Her bizarre patterns of thought and the strange behavior that followed were too serious a threat. "My only interest in Deszo is in his ability to help us hide Mila," I replied.

"Really, I find your timing suspicious." Anna rolled her shoulders and then lifted her hands to her hair, taking out the pins and tousling it. "He's leaving his wife."

I walked up to my sister and gently rested my hands on her shoulders and looked at our twin reflection in the mirror. "Anna, please try to remember that we have to protect Mila. I believe that the real you is still there beneath this insanity. I need you to understand that you cannot go back to the university anymore, because if they arrest you again, we may not be able to reach you in time. Or, they may come here, find Mila, and take both of you. Do you understand? Please, look at me and tell me you understand."

Chapter Sixteen

I woke to the smell of coffee. There was a light rap on my door and Mila came in carrying a tray. I pushed myself up in bed.

"Good morning!"

I smiled as she leaned over and kissed my cheek.

"Anna said that you were tired and needed to rest."

"What's Anna doing now?"

"She's in the kitchen writing. She says that she's working on a new poem."

I dipped the corner of my toast into the coffee, took a considered bite, and sighed at the small luxury. Anna was writing. I suppose I should feel thankful that she was doing that rather than giving lectures at the university. "And what are you up to this morning, besides making my breakfast?"

Mila blushed.

"What?" I persisted.

"Anna is teaching me to write poetry!"

My eyebrows arched in surprise. Mila longed to learn the mechanics of poetry. She'd been rebuffed in each previous approach to Anna.

Anna considered poetry an art form discovered, not taught. She was also very careful to limit her role as a teacher to the hours at the university. At home, she considered her time to be her own. She saw no students and usually remained in her bedroom at a small desk where she worked in solitude.

In years past, she would join my salons with a small group of writers, but more often than not she found them uninspiring, pedantic, and too self-absorbed to adequately provide the spotlight she commanded. When they'd ask her to read a work in progress, she'd retort that they could read the work when it was published. I wondered about Anna's sudden change of heart.

"You're working together?" Again, I dipped

the triangle of toast into the coffee and took a bite.

Mila nodded and glanced back toward the door as if anxious to return to Anna.

"Well then, go ahead."

Mila smiled and backed out of the room, closing the door behind her.

I swung my feet over the edge of the bed and moved the tray to my nightstand. I tapped my toes on the floor, considering what to do. It was eight a.m., and I had to meet Deszo at four o'clock. I nodded in thought and pushed myself off the bed.

I carried my breakfast tray to the kitchen. Anna was sitting at the kitchen table, Mila at her side. Together, they bent over a piece of paper filled with Mila's handwriting. They glanced up briefly as I entered the room and then back down at the paper. I walked to the sink, washed my plate and cup, and turned them upside down on the drain board.

Anna said to Mila, "You see, the end of this stanza should foreshadow the first line of the next. You're skipping ahead too quickly."

"Here?" Mila's voice was the siren of the

worshipful pupil. How quickly we draw in when satisfaction is imminent.

Anna smiled indulgently. "Yes dear, you must focus on the theme. Carry that through to the end."

It seemed all needs were met at that table. Mila crossed out a line, wrote another, and looked up at Anna hopefully.

"Yes," Anna nodded, and then shook her head. "Well no, not exactly. Rhyming words must be chosen carefully."

Looking toward the window, I saw that the breadcrumbs that I'd set out the night before were now gone and I smiled to myself, rueful that I'd missed the birds' arrival, wondering which ones had come today.

Anna continued. "Remember the poem I wrote this morning, about the birds that came to eat the breadcrumbs I'd set out? The black crow was a messenger."

I coughed back the desire to correct Anna's appropriation of my breadcrumbs and went to the stove to make more coffee. At the scrape of the kettle against the burner, Anna and Mila glanced expectantly at their empty cups. I took their cups from the table and rinsed them in the sink.

Mila's voice interrupted. "It's a symbol of the Nazis."

I folded my arms and leaned against the counter. Both women were wearing their robes over their pajamas. Had this meeting of the minds come up impromptu as they both wandered in to see who would make coffee?

Anna sighed, "No dear, the crow symbolizes the diseased psyche that has infected our people, causing them to succumb and separate."

I refilled their cups and left them to their reverie. I understood this desire to write, even before getting dressed. There was a time when I'd done the same.

I walked down the hall to my study and closed the door. Sitting at my desk, I pulled open the drawer and took out the red leather journal that belonged to Anna and the black leather folder containing a sheaf of papers comprising my edited version of her life. Carefully, I placed them side by side on the desktop and ran my fingers over the covers.

Looking back down at the contents of the drawer, I saw another leather folder. In blue. The white edges of paper stuck out like an obstinate tongue. I pulled the folder out and laid it on top of the work I'd completed of Anna's journal.

I hesitated before opening the cover. I saw my handwriting. Notes, bits of dialogue and description—it was the story I'd been working on when Anna had her nervous breakdown and had been asked to leave the university.

Tucked into the other sleeve of the folder was another slim, leather-bound book. My journal. I picked it up and flipped through the pages, reading bits here and there, of happier times and then the darkness that began with Max's death and, eventually, the coming of war. Finally, I came to the blank pages and stared at the creamy open space, wondering if I dared to bare my soul.

But who was I, if not a writer? A small voice inside me urged me on and I reached for the heavy, silver-capped fountain pen that had always been my favorite. Then I began writing, filling in the events of the past few days, solidifying my questions about Ilona, about Deszo, and also my fears for Mila.

Eventually, thoughts took the form of a letter, a conversation with God, albeit one-sided. Perhaps a prayer was a better description for the words that poured out of my heart to Him.

> *How can I keep Mila safe while my sister loses her grasp on reality? Will I have to choose between them? Where are You? And what of all the Jews? How can you stand by and watch the slaughter of your people, of so many innocents?*

I wrote as rapidly as my hand would travel across the page, without thought of grammar or spelling or even the splotches of ink that smudged the page as my left hand moved quickly across the freshly written words.

When I finished, I remained frustrated, but somehow I felt better. Although I was no closer to hearing an answer to my prayers for Mila's safety, I felt as if revealing my heart to God had somehow made my pleas more real. Perhaps the heartfelt authenticity of my words would help them reach

God's ears more quickly.

I sighed, feeling a bit more hopeful as I pulled the pages of a children's story out of the folder, and read through them quickly. How long ago and how out of place these gentle tales now seemed. How different those children's stories would sound in these days of endless fear. I picked up a pen that sat on the edge of my desk and a bright, white, blank sheet of paper. I began to compose a much different children's tale this time.

> *Long ago in the deep of the peaceful ocean swam a baby whale and its mother. It was summer, and they swam in the deep cold waters of the Arctic.*

I wouldn't allow myself to consider writing another gentle children's story until this war was over. I wouldn't lie to the children of our city by providing them with the false hope found in happy endings.

I was simply dictating my thoughts, just as I'd edited Anna's work over the past year. I became a shepherd of ideas, lining them up, culling the strays. I leaned over the pages as the words flowed out of my pen, as I considered a tale that conveyed the world we faced today.

Suddenly, Momma saw a school of sharks on the horizon. The sharks saw Herkimer and swam toward him.

I opened the right-hand drawer of the desk, pulled out two clean sheets of paper, and placed them to the side of the notes.

"Quick Herkimer, swim for the cave!"

It was too late. The sharks swarmed around them, and the deadly chase began. The sharks nipped at Herkimer in their attempt to separate him from his mother. They pushed the little whale further and further from his momma. And soon he couldn't see her at all, only a red cloud that seemed to spread through the water like a terrible shroud.

I lifted the pen from the paper and realized that the droplets on the paper were my tears. I shook my head and closed my eyes tight, forcing that final written scene from my mind's eyes.

"No, this has to stop." I whispered. I tapped the cap of the fountain pen against my lips as I pulled another crisp, white sheet of writing paper from the folder. Another thought grabbed me as I remembered the promise I'd made to myself on the night before Mila's abandonment. I promised I would write a different outcome to her story, one more certain than the one she currently faced.

Once upon a time, there was a beautiful, bright-eyed girl named Mila…

I wouldn't allow myself to feel the exhilaration of creating a hopeful future for Mila. Yet, I felt urgency with this story, an assured purpose in creating an alternate reality.

What better way to triumph over the negativity of the war, than to imagine Mila on a fantastic voyage across the sea? I ached for a long and happy life for my dear niece. I would create this for her in my story.

Just then, a thought occurred to me. If Anna came across this manuscript, she must not know what I am doing.

Once again I tapped the smooth cap of the

fountain pen against my lips as my eyes wandered to the odd assortment of objects on the bookshelves next to my desk.

There were mementos of my life. Pictures of Max, some in dusty, wooden frames, others unframed and propped against the spines of books. There were older, faded pictures of my parents, an icon of Mary holding the Baby Jesus, a small bouquet of dried red roses, and an outdated desk calendar in a silver frame.

I found the perfect spot to hide the story, up on the shelf, in amongst my other novels. I smiled and began to write again.

~*~

I could hear echoes of enthusiasm from Mila in the kitchen as she was just beginning her journey as a writer. What an inspiring way to counterbalance the awfulness of war. I regretted my earlier opinion that this was not the time for uplifting children's stories. What better time than now?

I sat this way for two hours. When I woke

from my reverie, it occurred to me that this was as it should be, as it had been in the past. It was the first normal morning that I'd had in months, or years.

Chapter Seventeen

How strange the war had made our lives. How artificial our days had become throwing off comforting routines, stealing the pleasure of completing simple tasks.

Anna had been right last night. She refused to let the war intrude upon her need to create. In fact, she'd used it as fuel, impetus for a new direction in her work. As she'd done with everything in her life, she'd turned even the most abnormal of situations inward toward her, where she was the center of the universe. I envied that.

Through my closed door, I heard the scrape of chairs in the kitchen, the murmur of voices as someone put the pot back on the stove for another cup of coffee. Their voices were friendly, though indistinct. I wondered at Anna's change. I glanced at the sky beyond our apartment window and saw that it was sunny. At least it would be for a few hours. I turned back to my work.

I wanted to remain in this cocoon of normalcy. I would resist the urge to put my pen down, bathe, and dress. I would stay a little longer and work.

My words drew me downward, and I began humming an old familiar tune. It was a waltz. One I often heard Max whistling. Each evening, the front door opened, and I would hear the stomping of his boots on the wood floors, a chuckle, and then the tune wafting down the hall as familiar as the smell of his pipe.

He would knock softly on the door of my study, enter, and stand behind my chair, placing his warm hands on my shoulders as he leaned over and kissed me on the cheek.

"How's the book coming?"

I would lean back, smile, and close my eyes as he kissed me again on the lips. "The story is coming along at its own slow pace."

"I can barely see what you've written, your eyes must be better than mine," he'd say. This was a gentle reminder to turn on the lamp and push back the encroaching darkness.

He'd pat me on the shoulders and then leave me, heading to the kitchen to confer with Marie about dinner. Shortly after, I would hear Max turn on the radio to listen to the news or classical music. That was the sign that Max had settled into his favorite chair to read the paper with a glass of sherry, but I had at least another hour's work to do before dinner.

I recalled an evening when I'd finished my writing for the day. I went into the living room, sat on the arm of Max's chair, and leaned into him as he put his arm around me. We sat in silence listening to music until Max told me that he'd seen Deszo earlier at a café. I knew the place. It was across the street from the stationers where I bought my pencils and pens.

They'd ordered sherry. Max took out a cigar, "I heard you received a censure from the university."

Deszo chuckled. "They dislike my corresponding with a professor from Hamburg."

"Our relations with the Germans are

complicated."

"We were exchanging research notes, Max."

"Political alliances are changing rapidly; you could lose your job."

Deszo took out a cigarette and lighted it, stared at the tip. "The smoke from a pile of leaves hides the fire beneath. The Germans will restore our borders, return our land, and strengthen our economy."

"Our alliance with the Germans will lead us into a war that will ruin our country," Max countered.

Deszo shrugged his shoulders and continued, "I've been invited to a symposium at their university. I will present a paper and participate in a panel discussion on the political and economic opportunities of an alliance between our countries."

"I hope you refused the invitation," Max said.

"On the contrary, my friend, I welcome the chance to share my ideas and, even better, to make contacts." Deszo blew out a long stream of smoke and then continued as he rolled the edge of his cigarette along the silver lip of the ashtray. "Their economic and military dominance cannot be ignored. I believe we are faced with the choice of joining them by invitation or by force, the latter would be much more unpleasant."

"By your reasoning, we either join the thieves in their crime or are robbed and murdered by them."

"Perhaps it is better to get rich than to get robbed," Deszo had replied, with no sign of irony.

On that day, the conversation had turned away from politics as it does between friends with differing opinions, and to the safer territory of wives and home.

I wondered then and wonder now if either man ever acknowledged the minefield that lay amidst this safe territory. After all, Deszo was having an affair with the identical twin of his best friend's wife. Did either man ever notice the scent of smoke coming from that pile of leaves?

In the silence of my study, I remembered the days when it was just the two of us living in this apartment. Before Max died. Before the entrance of

Ilona, Mila, and finally Anna. Before the war started, where instead of finding blue jays feasting on breadcrumbs, I had seen black crows.

Chapter Eighteen

The front door slammed, followed by the stomping of boots and laughter. I swallowed the tune I was humming and my heart skipped in anticipation of Max, and then sank at the impossibility and then leapt again wondering who had entered the apartment.

"Mila?" I turned toward the closed door. I heard more laughter and then footsteps coming toward my study. I looked back at the clock. It was three.

"Mila?" The handle turned and the door opened.

Mila's cheeks were flushed from the cold. She smiled warily, unwinding the blue wool scarf from around her neck. "Yes, Nana?"

"You…left the apartment." The words

staggered from my throat.

Her hands stopped, tightening around the tassels at the edge of the scarf. "We went for a walk."

"Where?"

"Just to the park," Mila didn't move from her position at the threshold of the room. "Were you working on Anna's journal?" she asked.

"Actually, I was working on a story of my own." I opened the drawer, lay the two leather folders side by side, and closed it. I tried to control the frustration in my voice. "You know you're not supposed to go out."

"Natalie, no one even noticed us." I turned and saw Anna standing behind Mila, her hands holding Mila's shoulders.

"You have no right to allow Mila to disobey me." I calculated the time it would take me to dress and reach Deszo. "How long have you been gone?"

"Two hours…maybe less," Anna replied.

"Only to the park? All that time? I don't believe you."

Anna sniffed, "It was cold, so we stopped to

have a cup of hot chocolate."

"Why don't you just take her down to the ghetto now?" My hands tightened around the arms of my chair. Mila cringed and I gasped. "I'm sorry Mila. I didn't mean it that way. I'm just trying to protect you. Don't you understand?"

Anna's eyes narrowed, and she steered Mila out of the room and closed the door behind her. I leapt from my chair and swung open the door following them down the hall to Mila's room. "It's for your own good. It's not safe out there."

"If anyone would have stopped us, which they didn't, I would have told them that she was my daughter."

Daughter? Last night, Anna regarded her as a nuisance. Was this Anna's jealous reprisal for Deszo's attention toward me? I looked from one to the other. They stood with their arms around each other's waist. Their alliance was a danger I hadn't anticipated.

~*~

The atmosphere had changed drastically since I'd last been here. I unbuttoned my coat and tugged the collar away from my neck, as the café was like a steam bath. Waitresses, trays aloft, turned from side to side like ballet dancers as they snaked their way from the counter to the waiting patrons.

I followed one of them into the throng. The tables overflowed with people huddled over small cups of ersatz-Turkish coffee, more chicory than coffee, and their heads bobbing up and down as they carried on conversations and surreptitiously watched people at other tables do the same.

A man suddenly pulled back from his table and into my path. I stopped, grabbed my coat to my middle and turned sideways as he grunted an excuse and brushed by me.

I didn't want to call attention to myself. There were too many uniforms. I couldn't make out the faces through the tobacco smoke that hung in clouds over the tables, but it was clear that the Germans had come to occupy this place as easily as our country.

I prayed Deszo had come alone. A rivulet of cold sweat slipped between my shoulder blades. There was another room beyond the heavy maroon curtains, shielded from view.

I'd never seen them closed before. I could hear the laughter of men, and the guttural cadence of German coming from behind the curtain. I turned around surveying the main room.

There, finally, was Deszo was leaning back in his chair surveying the room like a ringmaster, smoking. I wondered how long he'd been watching me. He signaled me with a wave of his hand and stood as I approached.

"Not our usual crowd is it?" Deszo took my coat and laid it over the chair between us. He caught the eye of the waitress and ordered another cup of coffee.

I sat down and slowly took off my gloves, studying my hands. "I don't like being here."

Deszo smirked and shrugged. "For the most part, they're harmless. At least in here." The clank of his glass against the saucer brought my eyes to his. "Any more unexpected visitors?"

I shuddered remembering the look on the young soldier's face as he stood just outside our door last night. I shook my head.

"How is Anna today?"

I glanced at a bad reproduction of a Titian painting on the wall behind us, and then back at Deszo. "She took Mila out while I was writing."

Deszo frowned. "Where did they go?"

"Anna said they went for a walk in the park and then stopped for hot chocolate." I leaned back and waited as the waitress put a cup of coffee in front of me. "But that's not the point is it?"

"Strange." A bemused smile tugged at the corner of his mouth. "Anna's never shown the slightest interest in Mila."

"And she decided to teach her poetry this morning."

"Who can understand Anna? Well, at least Mila doesn't look…like her father."

"But if she's seen by one of our neighbors—there was the incident with Mrs. Nyugati."

"You think she'd turn in Mila."

"Of course. To protect her shop from further

persecution."

"Self-preservation." Deszo nodded and his blue eyes followed my hands. "We shouldn't be surprised. So Mila should be moved."

As the woman at the next table began to flirt with the German officer sitting next to her, I whispered, "What will she think if I abandon her to strangers?"

"Lean back and relax Natalie." Deszo smiled and lifted his cup to his lips. "Remember where you are. We are discussing nothing more than the weather."

I made an effort to relax my shoulders and return his smile. "She must stay with us." I laughed lightly.

Deszo joined in the chuckle and added, "Not safely."

Nodding toward the maroon curtains, I sighed, "This silliness can't go on much longer. Aren't our friends expected soon?"

"The party could go on and on." He tapped the edge of the saucer restlessly. "Regardless, they will continue to send our relatives on holiday.

They're single-minded in their generosity."

The woman at the next table squealed, "Stop it, Gunter!"

I met the woman's gaze and then quickly averted my eyes. "It's not just them. Our own are just as responsible."

I turned back for a second glance. She was Hungarian. A young woman, attractively dressed, her hair carefully rolled under and lipstick freshly applied to an ample mouth. I wondered if her boyfriend or husband valiantly fought at the front. What circumstances had compelled her to offer herself in this way? Safety? shelter? food? Or was it as simple as loneliness.

"They've become emboldened by the presence of our new guests."

"Where can Mila go?"

"There are homes. But, they're overcrowded, filthy, with minimal food."

"Impossible."

The woman whispered something to her companion. The German officer looked at me, our eyes met. An unwelcome spark of physical attraction made my cheeks flush, and his look made it clear that he acknowledged my reaction. I smoothed my hair, his handsome features creased in a smile and I quickly looked away.

"Do you have any friends you could send her to? Someone you trust."

The enemy could be handsome. I shook the image of Gunter's smile from my mind and answered Deszo. "Friends, yes. But none that I could ask...no. That won't work."

"Let me speak to my wife. Maybe she would…"

"Don't be ridiculous."

"Then let me think further. In the meantime, keep Mila inside."

"What if I went with Mila?"

"Where?"

"Anywhere. Let me go with her to one of those houses."

"And leave Anna alone?"

"Damn it! Why can't Anna take care of herself?"

"You know why."

I knew better than Deszo what it was like to live with Anna's erratic swings between hysteria and calm, her unpredictable lashing out.

There was a scrape of a chair and then the German was standing over us. "Excuse me," he said, bowing slightly. "Could you spare a cigarette?"

Deszo paused and then tapped one out from the pack next to his cup. "Of course. Do you need a light?"

He offered his lighter, and the German leaned over bringing the cigarette close to the flame. He inhaled deeply and then straightened and smiled at me, exhaling a stream of smoke. "Thank you. I'm sorry to interrupt your conversation, you were so engrossed."

I fumbled with the scarf I held in my lap, "Just friends."

The German smiled and examined the ash of his cigarette. "Would you like to join my friends at our table?"

Would Deszo feel compelled to consent? "Thank you, no."

Gunter's eyes searched my face and then wandered down the length of my body. "Are you sure I can't convince you?"

I blushed at the warmth that coursed through me, frightened that my body could react this way to an officer who would just as easily kill my niece as seduce me.

"Certainly your conversation can't be that important." He offered me his hand, and I took it but remained seated.

"I'm sorry, but I have to go soon."

"Something more interesting waiting at home?" The strength of his fingers made me gasp as he enclosed his hand in mine.

I pulled my hand away and quickly returned it to my lap.

"Gunter! I'm getting lonely!" The woman's scornful stare clearly stated her territorial intentions.

Once again, Gunter bowed from the waist, his eyes never leaving mine, "Perhaps I'll have the pleasure of your company another time."

He released my hand slowly, lingering at my

fingertips. He returned to his table and quieted his companion with a whispered message in her ear. I shivered feeling his breath against my neck. My hands trembled as he continued to watch me even though his companion was doing her best to distract him by kissing his cheek and pressing into him.

"Deszo, I must go," I said reaching for my coat.

"Not unless you want to make him suspicious." Deszo signaled the waitress for two more cups of coffee. "Sit back, smile and pretend we really are just two old friends."

I couldn't stop the trembling in my hands. "Yes, but I really should get home."

"I think we should finish our conversation about Anna first."

I glanced over at the German officer, relieved to find that the woman's eager hands had finally distracted him. "We can find someone to take Anna. Then I would be free to go with Mila."

"You'll choose Mila over Anna?"

"A plan for both." I splayed my hands on the table as if mapping out the solution.

"There's no telling what Anna would say." Deszo sat back and lighted another cigarette. "After all, she'll think she's been betrayed by you."

"You think it's a betrayal?"

"She's your sister."

"A compromise. Anna deserves a holiday in the country, and then Mila and I will leave together."

Deszo squinted as he exhaled a blue plume of smoke. "Why not go with Anna?"

"It will only work if she doesn't know where we are."

Deszo rolled the ash of the cigarette along the edge of the saucer. After a moment he said, "Then we'll find a place to take Anna, get her there, and convince her to stay, without you."

"Depending on her state of mind, it will either be easy or impossible," I replied, but my eyes focused again on the German. His hair was a paler blonde than my own. I guessed that we were the same age, though his face bore the evidence of someone who has seen death more often and more closely. It had been so long since I'd felt the touch of a man.

"Natalie, I'm concerned that this is too much for you." Deszo reached for my hand. Behind me, someone began humming. The flirt had invited Gunter to join her in a song, and they were joined by a group of soldiers who'd just entered the cafe.

"Natalie."

I put up my hand to stop him. "Deszo, don't. Don't tell me what you are feeling."

"But..."

"No! No! You have no right."

I grabbed my coat and stood. Gunter stood at the same time. I gasped, and his table went silent and turned in our direction. I clutched my throat, as he tipped his cap and smiled. I hurried for the exit.

The street was crowded with people on their way home. A man in a heavy blue wool overcoat brushed past me, and I caught a whiff of cologne.

My head snapped up, "Max!" My husband's name slipped from my lips as I watched the back of the coat disappear into the throng ahead of me.

I stopped and let the crowd swarm around me.

My head swam with Deszo's accusations that I was betraying Anna. I thought of Mila and wondered how I would be able to keep her from being swept into the vortex of the war. Anna. Gunter. My stomach roiled. The thought of going back to the apartment repulsed me. I was as sick of those four walls as Mila and Anna. I turned and walked in the opposite direction.

Chapter Nineteen

Within an hour, I found myself standing in front of carved, wrought-iron gates that enclosed a small, secluded cemetery. The heavy latch gave way as I pushed against it.

In the twilight, I made my way along the path between rows and rows of old plots. The tombstones stood bent and weathered with age, and withered flowers lay in sullen heaps. Max was buried in one of the last available plots in the back corner, near a garden wall which was overshadowed by buildings on either side. There would be no room for my grave next to his.

I found Max's gravestone and knelt beside it. My fingers touched the engraved words of his name. Brushing aside the withered remnants of leaves, I leaned over, laid my head against the cold stone, and embraced its rough surface with my arms. I curled myself around the gravestone and held it as if I were embracing Max, the uneven ground jabbing my legs beneath the edge of my coat. I remembered his appearance in my dream and hoped to find him here.

"What should I do, Max?"

"What would you do?"

"Deszo was always your best friend. Of course, I can trust him. Perhaps I'm only imagining his interest in me. I know, I know, you always said it was a good thing you'd proposed first. I don't think Deszo's was serious, do you? I mean back then, we were all young and foolish, and we were always playing games. You remember, don't you?"

"But what do I do now? You're not here! I don't like being responsible for all these people. And the German, Max. You forgive me for those thoughts don't you? I couldn't help it. I am only human. No, I know that's no excuse. Oh God, I am wicked. Max, am I so bad? I never considered another man when you were alive. Now, now, I am attracted to the same man who would eagerly kill our niece. God help me. I want to go away. I want to be with you, Max."

Suddenly, my face was shoved against the ground. A hand was rummaging through the pocket of my coat. I screamed and rolled to my side to sit up. He slapped me hard, my head slammed against the headstone and my ears rang against the shock. I screamed—but he put his hand over my mouth.

"Give me your money." The teenager hovering over me stank of liquor. His face was pockmarked, his hair greasy and dark, his clothes bore the filth of the homeless.

I cried out and managed to kick out at his crotch. He cursed and reared back to hit me again. Just then, another young man standing over him joined him. The other boy pulled my assailant off me and yelled, "Get back!"

"I'll kill her," the first one said.

"Off!" The other boy shoved him aside and bent over me, grasping my chin, turning my face into the dim light from a building adjacent to the graveyard. He said, "I know her."

"You know her."

"Yes!"

"She'll turn us in to the police!"

"She won't."

I struggled to sit up. The boy who'd hit me backed into the shadows. The other boy knelt beside me, brushed off my coat, and reached for my arm to help me up.

"You shouldn't be here alone," he said.

I pushed him away, "I can see that visiting the dead is dangerous."

"Don't you remember me?"

In the dim light his features became familiar. How strange that the thief was now my savior. "Jozef."

"Yes." He retrieved my scarf from the ground and handed it to me.

I wound the scarf around my neck and buttoned my coat. Gingerly, I touched my cheek, the skin hot beneath my fingertips. "You don't limit your thievery to homes."

"A well-dressed woman sitting in an empty cemetery is too tempting a target." Jozef looked over at his accomplice, "I'll meet you later."

The other boy hesitated, "You'd better share whatever you get," and then moved off toward the entrance.

Jozef turned back to me. "What are you doing here?"

"Visiting my husband," I said.

"How's the girl?"

"You mean Mila. She's fine."

"Come on, let's get out of here," Jozef reached for my arm. "I'll walk you home."

"Oh, so you can steal more from me?" I tried to wrest my arm from his grasp, but he held me tightly.

Jozef shook his head, "No, so someone else doesn't rob you on the way home. It's getting dark. You're stupid to be out alone."

"Then let go of me."

"As you wish," he said, releasing my arm. "I was just trying to help."

The narrow path between the headstones was almost impossible to make out as a canopy of branches overhead blocked the light. I stumbled over a rock on the path and Jozef grabbed my arm.

At the entrance to the cemetery I paused, "I can get home by myself."

"I think you better let me take you."

I wasn't sure if his tone contained threat or concern. He had saved me from certain death from his friend. On the other hand, what if, as his friend had intimated, Jozef had no plans of sharing a bigger haul?

"That's not necessary."

"Is your niece still looking for a safe place to hide?"

I paused, not certain whether to answer him truthfully. "She's gone."

Jozef searched my eyes and then a thin smile spread across his face. "Of course, I'm sure it was easy."

"I have friends," I replied defensively.

Jozef fell into step next to me. "Then you won't mind if I escort you home. For your safety."

I stopped again and turned to toward him. "What do you want? Money? Blackmail? To steal my possessions? I'm sorry I won't let you. If you're hungry, I'll give you the small amount of money I have in my pocket, and you can buy food. I have nothing more to offer you."

"You're drawing attention to yourself. You really know nothing about how to conduct yourself in the street, do you?" Jozef took my arm and steered me down the sidewalk.

I tore my arm away from him. "You are the enemy."

Jozef shook his head. "I'm a thief by necessity. Mrs. Nyugati is more dangerous to you than I could ever be."

I stopped. Again, Jozef took my arm and continued to walk.

"What do you know about Mrs. Nyugati?" I asked.

"She's one of my customers," Jozef said. "Actually her husband is. I buy them things for their store that they couldn't get otherwise."

"What has she said?"

"She talks about the money she's been offered to turn in people who are hiding Jews. She's mentioned you."

I attempted to break free from Jozef, but his grip was too tight. "When did she say this?"

"This afternoon."

"When?"

He shrugged. "About the time she saw Mila and your sister leaving the apartment and walking by her store."

"Oh God," I whispered.

"You're lucky she only told me and not the Nazi soldier that was in the shop at the same time."

I began to hurry toward home. "How do you know she didn't tell him?"

Jozef's arm slowed me. "Remember the point is not to draw attention to yourself."

"How do you know she didn't tell the Nazi?"

"Because I paid her off."

"I don't believe you!"

He tightened his grip around my arm and hissed, "Quiet."

"You don't have that kind of money," I said bowing my head.

Jozef chuckled. "I probably have more money than you do. I'm a businessman. I profit from the war."

"You're just a young boy."

"I'm fifteen. Don't be so naive," Jozef chuffed.

My head was reeling trying to digest everything he'd said, trying to pick the truth from the lies. "Why did you pay her off?"

"Why do you think?"

"Because you believe you can make more by coming to me."

Jozef didn't reply, but continued to walk me down the street toward my apartment. I tried to imagine a scenario that would get me out of this situation. I would pay anything he asked to keep his silence. I just wondered if I had enough money. This might be the first of many payments I would have to make to him.

"Tell me how much you want," I repeated.

"You are protecting your niece only because her mother left her. Is that right?"

"Yes. Why is that so strange?"

"Why risk your life for her?"

"Because I love her."

"Mrs. Nyugati says the Jews killed Christ so

it's God's retribution that they face now."

"That's ridiculous. God doesn't stoop to the petty revenge of man. Hitler's a charlatan using the prejudices of his people to further his own wicked agenda."

"He's found a lot to follow him."

"Yes, but why did you pay off Mrs. Nyugati? And how do you know that she still won't turn in Mila to the Nazis? She could get paid twice."

"She won't tell the Nazis because she knows that if she does I will stop being her supplier. She also knows that the cost of betraying me is a lot worse than money."

"What would you do?"

"Let's just say that money couldn't repair it."

I had a new appreciation of Jozef, although I knew he was warning me as well as informing. A boy his age hadn't become a businessman by doing things according to the rules. I imagined there were exceptionally brutal methods required to operate in his chosen profession.

"But still," I asked, careful now. "Why pay her off on our behalf?"

"If she informs to the Nazis once, they'll come back to her for information again and again. I might be her next pay-off."

"But she needs you," I countered.

"She's greedy, which makes her thinking predictable."

"You want me to believe that you paid for Mila's safety, to protect yourself?"

Jozef looked at me and cocked an eyebrow. "You don't believe that do you."

"No."

"You know Deszo Eckhart."

There were too many coincidences. I couldn't imagine how Jozef would know Deszo, or why Jozef would be interested in him. What could Deszo possibly have to offer this street thug? How could their paths have ever crossed? I remained silent.

Jozef prompted, "You had coffee with him."

"You've been following me!"

This time it was Jozef's turn to remain silent. He dug his hands into his pockets and glanced out toward the street traffic.

"Then why do you ask if I know him? Obviously if you saw me meet with him you know that I do."

"I don't know how well you know him."

"That's none of your concern."

"There are other ways for me to find out," Jozef warned.

"What do you want with Deszo?"

Jozef squared his shoulders as if to look older and more mature. "I think he and I could help one another."

I wanted to laugh. How could this young thug believe that he could have anything to do with Deszo? They were entirely different. Deszo was a well-educated, cultured man from an upper-class background. He was politically neutral, and not prone to intrigue. His most daring escapade, as far as I knew, was his long affair with my sister.

"Deszo is a professor. Are you planning to join the university? You'd like him to help you get in."

Jozef laughed. "You know I'm too young to attend university. And in the middle of a war, education of that sort is a waste of time."

"Then how do you imagine Deszo could help you?"

"It's Deszo's other work that I'm interested in."

"I am not aware that Deszo has any other work than his job at the University. But if you know differently, why don't you go to him yourself?"

"He would never listen to someone like me. I need an introduction."

"Leverage," I said turning to look at him with new understanding. "You need Deszo to have a reason to help you and I am that reason."

Jozef shrugged. "You're an incentive."

"And my incentive is Mila."

"It's a small thing I'm asking," Jozef replied.

I hadn't noticed how close were to home. I looked up and saw my apartment building on the next block. "I need to think about it."

Jozef nodded and said, "There's nothing to think about. I want to meet Deszo. It's a simple request."

"But you haven't told me what the purpose of your meeting would be."

"You don't need to know."

"Deszo is a friend of mine," I warned. "I'm not going to put him in harm's way for you. Or anyone else."

"He's already in harm's way."

I couldn't recall anything that hinted at Deszo's participation in any organization that would put him in jeopardy. In fact, Max used to tease him about his ardent disdain for the student organizations against the government. "In what way?" I asked Jozef.

"He works with the Nazis."

I was stunned, "You mean he's a collaborator?"

"It's more complicated than that."

"How do you know? You told me you didn't know him."

"I hear things."

I shook my head. This was unbelievable. "You're a thief!"

"I am a businessman," Jozef said defensively. "It is my business to know where opportunities are, and how I can take advantage of them."

"You could get yourself killed."

He smiled. "So, you'd like to take care of me too."

"Tell me what you know of Deszo's work," I demanded.

"He is in contact with some German officers," Jozef explained. "And I have some talks from time to time with those officers."

"What could you be talking to them about? Are you working for them? How do I know that you won't tell them about Mila?"

"Not that kind of work. I have no interest in helping them round up Jews."

"Then what?"

"They are new in town," he laughed. "They want to find friends. Female friends."

"You're a pimp as well as a thief."

"I simply make introductions. The girls know what is expected of them. They have a variety of reasons to do what they do."

"Yes, but without your help it wouldn't be so easy."

Jozef sighed as if he was exasperated by her naiveté, but there was also a defensive note in his reply. "If it wasn't me, it would be someone else."

My head was reeling. This was ridiculous. A black sedan bearing Nazi flags slowly drove by. It stopped, and the rear window rolled down.

A young soldier stuck his head out the window and gestured toward us. "Where are you two going so late at night?"

"We're on our way home," Jozef answered.

"You're breaking curfew," the soldier said. "Let me see your papers."

I reached in my coat pocket, but Jozef stopped me.

"It's not so late, is it?" Jozef looked toward the horizon as if he expected to see the sun just setting. He then made a show of looking at this wrist. "I must have left my watch at home!"

"Your papers!" The soldier demanded.

Jozef held up his hands as if to show that he was unarmed. "Can't a man take a stroll with his girlfriend?"

The soldier turned from me to Jozef and laughed. He turned to his companion in the car, and I heard the laughter of another man. "She's too old for you! Not for us!"

I shivered. Was this how Jozef got women for the Germans? I pulled my coat closed and took a step backwards.

The German's eyes traced my body from top to bottom. He held out his hand toward me, and I shook my head. "Why don't you join us for a drink?"

"No, thank you." I tried to sound pleasant, but my voice was shaking.

"It's not a suggestion," he retorted. "You wouldn't be wise to turn us down!"

Instinctively, I glanced toward my apartment building. It was within one block, I could see the doorway from where I was standing.

The officer followed my gaze. "You live there?"

"No," I gasped. "I was on my way to visit a friend."

He nodded toward Jozef, "He said you were on your way home. So who's lying?"

I stared at the ground and wondered if my legs would continue to hold me. How could I have been so stupid? If they followed us back to the apartment it would be my fault.

"Maybe you have more friends to entertain us," the soldier gestured toward my building, "over there."

"No!" I exclaimed. "I was going to visit an old friend of my husband's."

"A lady friend?" Laughter emanated from the backseat.

"No, of course not, a gentleman."

"Ah, a gentleman…you must be lonely," the soldier said, with a wink. "Come with us and you will be less lonely."

"I have a better idea."

Jozef stepped up to the car and leaned over placing his hand on the windowsill as if he and the officer were old acquaintances. He spoke in a low tone so that I was unable to hear his conversation. His face turned away from me, but I could see the expression of the German soldier's face change from stern accusation to recognition, and then a sly smile.

He nodded several times and then turned back

to his companion in the back seat to consult with him. Jozef said something and pointed down the street in the opposite direction from my home. The German followed his gesture and then back at me as if trying to decide.

Jozef took a roll of money from his pocket and pushed it toward the soldier. The German considered the money and then Jozef. He shook his head and pushed the money away.

He frowned and pointed to me and then said something as if bargaining. Jozef shook his head and put both his hands on the window ledge blocking me from the view of the German. He gestured down the street and tried to force his money toward the German. He said something and then the two of them laughed.

Finally, Jozef stepped back from the car and made a mock salute. The German returned the salute and then blowing a kiss in my direction, he sat back in his seat and rolled up the window. I held my breath as the car made a U-turn and slowly drove down the street.

Jozef walked back to me and took my arm.

"Let's get out of here."

"What did you say to them?"

"You don't need to know, the outcome is obvious."

He walked me to the steps of my building. I was surprised when he stopped.

"Thank you for your help," I said. "This is the second time tonight you've come to my rescue."

Jozef shrugged and then stared at the windows of my apartment. "They'd think nothing of taking a girl of Mila's age and using her for their own entertainment instead of sending her to the ghetto."

I was shocked and yet I knew he was right. "What can I do?"

He hesitated, continuing to look at the windows and then back at me. "I will come to your apartment tomorrow."

"When?" I asked. "I have to go out tomorrow."

"To meet Deszo?"

I wanted to lie. My hesitation gave me away instead.

"Take me to your meeting with Deszo."

"How do I know that you won't blackmail

both of us?"

"You don't," Jozef said. "Besides, if I were going to do that, I wouldn't tell you anyway."

Chapter Twenty

I hurried up the stairs trying at once to absorb Jozef's demands while wondering if Mila and Anna were safe. At the first floor landing, I noticed Miss Szep's door was ajar. I paused, undecided as to what to do. She lived alone, with no living relatives that I knew of.

Even at her age and given the food shortages associated with the war, she'd remained mentally sharp and relatively healthy. Therefore, it was unlike Miss Szep to leave the door unlocked. She rarely went out anymore. Mr. Nyugati sent his son Michael once a week to deliver her a small bag of groceries.

When I put my hand on the doorknob to pull the door closed, it resisted as if someone was holding it from the other side. I heard Miss Szep talking to her cat and then her head popped out from behind the door.

"Come in!" she whispered, opening the door and motioning toward me.

"I'm sorry, I truly can't. I have to get upstairs to my sister."

Miss Szep looked down the stairs and then up towards my apartment. "I need to talk to you. Don't worry they're both upstairs."

"How do you know?" Then I nodded. Miss Szep's apartment was directly beneath ours, and she was able to hear our movements. From her sentry post at her front window, I knew she monitored the comings and goings of the building's occupants and their guests.

I stepped into her foyer and squinted, adjusting my eyes to the dark hallway. "Have you lost your electricity?"

"No, it works as well any anyone else's," she replied, taking my hand and leading me toward her sitting room. "I just don't like to use it much at night. It's too easy to see in my windows from the street."

I held back a smile knowing that the darkened room allowed her to watch the street undetected. "You're sure that Mila and Anna are both upstairs?"

"No one's left the apartment since you left this afternoon. I saw them go out and come back before that. You should tell them it isn't safe."

"They know," I said. "They just..."

"Yes, yes," Miss Szep said leading me to a chair and motioning that I should sit. "Your sister is the restless type."

"She sometimes lets her passion to help the students overcome her judgment," I offered.

Miss Szep was a professor of chemistry at the university until she retired. She was also an ardent fan of Anna's poetry. Before her illness, Anna often came downstairs and sat with Miss Szep, reading her latest poems, discussing poetry, drinking tea and eating the fresh poppy seed rolls that Miss Szep baked.

During the past year, Anna's visits had become increasingly infrequent. There were days when she'd ask me who lived downstairs since Miss

Szep's death. And then the following week she'd come out of the bath and tell me she'd just had the nicest cup of coffee with Miss Szep, when of course, Anna hadn't left the apartment all day.

"Anna shouldn't worry about the students," Miss Szep said, wearily sinking into a chair across from me. "The students will take care of themselves. If anything, they will use her former stature to raise that of their cause, and then when her illness makes her inconvenient, they will abandon her. This is nothing new."

I nodded, knowing she was right. The students felt the revolution was theirs because only a young mind was uncorrupted. Yet, when the police had dragged Anna from the classroom, they'd cheered her call to arms. When she was taken to the Dean's office, they'd scurried away like mice.

Solidarity was admirable, but loyalty was the person standing next to you when the devil came to call.

Although I trusted Miss Szep's assurance that Mila and Anna were upstairs, I longed to see for myself rather than sit here discussing politics.

"Miss Szep was there something you needed?"

"I wanted to make you an offer," she said.

My heart skipped a beat. "What?"

"I wanted to offer you the use of my apartment for Mila."

"Miss Szep, I would never endanger you like that."

"Nonsense," she replied. "She would be safer here than in your apartment."

"For a time," I agreed. "But if they came to search our apartment first, yours would be searched second. They would tear this building apart if they thought there were any chance she was hiding here."

"But you can't continue to hide her in your apartment," she argued. "It's just a matter of time before they come for her. There are others who know she's here."

"You mean Mrs. Nyugati," I said.

Miss Szep nodded. "I won't say a word. I already know about her. I know that you are dependent upon the kindness of Mr. Nyugati for your groceries. I wouldn't do anything to jeopardize that."

Miss Szep smiled. "I know you wouldn't. I just wish there was something I could do to help you. Your family has always been exceedingly kind to me."

"I'm trying to find a safe place to take Mila and myself."

"Together?"

"Yes." I quickly added, "Anna will go to stay with a friend. I wouldn't leave her here alone."

"Do you know where you will go?"

"No," I replied. "I have to contact some of Anna's old friends. There are so few that will have anything to do with her anymore. She alienated many of them before she left the university."

"And you and Mila?"

"That will be more difficult. I think it would be best for us to go where we are not known."

"I know someone in the country."

"I've heard they have it worse than we do here," I said. "With fewer people to see their brutality, the Nazis are committing greater atrocities in the smaller villages than they would ever contemplate here."

"No, the only reason we are not seeing the same massacres here is that they are finally meeting more resistance from the Allies, and their attention is distracted by the Russians." She shrugged her shoulders. "And they've just arrived in our city. Just wait. They haven't given up their old tricks. They simply haven't had time to implement them. Budapest will see the same that others have seen."

I shivered. "Then it is more urgent that I take Mila away." Her remark about the Russians planted a thought in my head.

"Why not hide her here in the Buda? I have a friend, Mrs. Gödel, she has a home, and..."

"No, I don't want to put your friend in danger."

"But you admitted yourself that you need to go where no one knows you. She lives in a different neighborhood. Up in the hills. You could be her daughter. Or a niece."

It was tempting. I knew the woman. I had no doubt she would accept Mrs. Szep's suggestion, or that she would keep our secret safe. However, I wasn't familiar with the attitude of her neighbors; would they become suspicious of the timing of our arrival?

"Let me think about it," I said.

"How is it possible for you to be so different from your twin? Living in the same house. How is this possible?"

I shook my head. "The answer would take too long to explain, Mrs. Szep." I put my hands on my knees and stood up. "But now I have to go upstairs to see how my sister and niece are doing."

"Think about my offer," she said.

"Thank you, I will," I said. "In the meantime, please come up and visit us. I know Anna and Mila would welcome the company."

I went over to the chair where Mrs. Szep was sitting and leaned down and kissed her forehead. "Please come and visit."

Mrs. Szep smiled and nodded. "I'll bring some of Anna's favorite pastry. Maybe that will help her feel better."

I retraced my steps down the corridor to the front door and stepped back into the stairway, closing the door behind me. I hoped Mrs. Szep wouldn't forget to lock it before she went to bed. I looked up at the entrance to my apartment on the next landing and slowly began to climb the stairs.

Chapter Twenty-One

There was a time when evening meant quiet community. I could look up from my book and see Anna at the doorway smiling as she waved good-bye on her way out to spend the evening with Deszo at the opera.

I would hear Mila down the hall, perhaps with a friend from school visiting, talking conspiratorially in her bedroom about some cute boy's antics in class that day as they made some effort to get through their nightly homework. We were still a community of women then. Ilona and her husband were rarely around.

Still, I missed my husband. Anna or Mila could never fill the intimacy of understanding that Max and I shared. They filled the void he left with a different kind of love. We shared meals together. Sat and drank coffee afterwards, talked and more importantly—laughed.

Now that community had split apart. I entered the apartment and found it quiet. I walked to the kitchen and saw the dishes neatly stacked to dry on the washboard. There was no pot of soup warming for me on the stove, though the smell of the meal remained in the air. My stomach rumbled, reminding me that it had been hours since I'd last eaten.

I walked down the hall. The doors to Mila and Anna's rooms were open. Mila was sitting on her bed, leaning against the headboard reading. Anna's room was empty.

"Where is Anna?" I asked.

Mila looked up from her book and said, "Where were you for so long?"

"I had a meeting," I replied. "Where is Anna?"

"You got mad at us and we were only gone a couple hours." Mila's voice became a pout. "You're a hypocrite."

"Mila!" I tried fruitlessly to contain my rising

anger. She'd never been so arrogantly defiant before. Clearly, this was Anna's influence. I can imagine the bitter recriminations Anna must have filled her head with while I was gone. "Mila, my absence and yours are two different things. Now, tell me where is Anna?"

Mila hugged herself and turned to the wall. "Find her yourself."

"Where did she go?"

Mila merely shrugged. Miss Szep had assured me that neither Mila nor Anna had left the apartment since my departure to meet Deszo. Then again, she was an old woman. It was likely that she could have been napping when Anna left the house.

"Mila you must tell me where Anna went." I walked over to her bed and grabbed her chin, turning her to face me. "Tell me what happened."

Mila's eyes filled with tears, and she was visibly frightened of me. I recoiled and dropped my hand. "I'm sorry Mila. You know she's not well, it's not safe for women out on the streets at night."

I sat down on the edge of her bed and took her hand in both of mine. "I know how difficult this is to understand. I know that I seem like a different person to you. I haven't changed."

"You have!"

"No honey, I haven't changed, the circumstances…"

"Even Anna says you've changed!"

I sighed, prolonging the argument would be fruitless. "You're probably right. I'm not the same person that I was a week ago." I needed to find some way to reach Mila. "It's just that so much has happened. I'm trying to find a way to keep you safe since…"

"Since Momma left."

"Yes, since your mother left. I wasn't prepared for that. I was hoping that she would take you with her, so that you'd be safe too."

"And you can't understand why she didn't?"

"Can you?" I looked into Mila's eyes, scarred by pain since the scene at the train station.

"She never loved me like you did."

"Like I still do."

"But you're not so nice now. Maybe you'll..."

"Leave you too?" I softened my voice, caught by grief that my darling child, yes— my child--

that's how I'd always thought of her. Ilona knew that and as much as she'd considered Mila a burden, she resented my relationship with her daughter as if I were a trespasser. "I will never leave you Mila."

Mila wiped an angry tear from her eye. She hugged me tightly. I held her to my chest and let her cry for the first time since her mother had left.

I whispered in her hair, "What happened tonight, after I left?"

"Anna went to your study. She shut the door."

Mila's sentences came out in slow gulps in between her breaths from crying. "She stayed in there for a while. And then she came out carrying some books, they looked like notebooks."

I held my breath, I could feel my heart pounding through my shirt. I willed myself to stay and listen to the rest of the story instead of running to my study to confirm my suspicions. "What did she say, Mila?"

"She was mad," Mila replied looking away. "She said that you'd betrayed her. That you were going to run off with Deszo and leave us alone."

"Did she say anything else? Did she say where she was going?"

Mila remained silent. I couldn't decide whether she was recalling Anna's words or choosing which ones to tell me. "Mila, please, this is important! Anna could be in danger!"

"She said that you'd betrayed her twice. She said you weren't working on her journals, you were working on your own stories because you were jealous of her."

I shook my head and yet I could clearly imagine Anna's reasoning. I'd given up writing in the early years of my marriage. And then, at my husband's insistence, I'd begun again. I chose children's stories knowing they were well out of the realm of Anna's interest. I wrote in obscurity for years, most of my stories published with the assistance of Max's money rather than public interest. But slowly, I had earned a following.

My popularity grew. There were requests to

publish some stories in Germany, then France, and even England, just before the war broke out. Secretly, I'd even begun to hope that my writing would eventually find its way to that most coveted market, America.

I had once again begun to surpass Anna in recognition. And then Max died. And so did my voice.

After three years of silence, there was an offer from a publisher who wanted me to contribute an original children's story to an anthology that would be published internationally as part of a peace initiative to show that artists of all countries could work cooperatively. It would have been the international exposure that Max and I had often talked about. Coincidently, it was also at this time that Anna suggested I edit her journals instead returning to my own work.

"Did Anna say where she was going?"

Mila shook her head.

"How was she dressed?"

Mila furrowed her brow as if wondering why I would ask such a simple-minded question.

"She went to her room and put on a dress. I watched her put on her make-up. I asked her where she was going, but she just laughed and said she was going to take care of things. Then she went down the hall and put on her coat and left."

"Which dress she was wearing?"

"It looked like one of the dresses she wore when she went out dancing."

I shut my eyes and sighed. Now I knew where she'd gone.

I opened my eyes and grasped Mila's hands. "I have to go out to find Anna. I don't want you to stay here alone. Will you go down to Miss Szep's? You can spend the night there, and I'll come and get you in the morning."

Mila pulled her hands out of my grasp. "What if something happens to you and Anna? What if you don't come back?"

There was no point in giving her false assurances. We both knew it was possible that anything could happen tonight.

"If that happens, Miss Szep has a friend you can stay with. You'll be safe with her. And I will come and find you there and bring you home."

Mila looked doubtful, but she was old enough to understand how serious the situation was with Anna alone and possibly disclosing information that could harm us all. She pushed the covers down and swung her legs over the side of the bed.

"That's my girl!" I tried to smile, to keep my voice light. "Now, take some clothes to wear tomorrow, you can just put your robe over your pajamas. And take a good book to read to her cat."

Chapter Twenty-Two

I left Mila and walked down the hall to my study. Papers were strewn across my desk. I shoved them aside, underneath was my journal, open to the entry I'd made this morning.

I look in the mirror and I see my sister. I am afraid that I will become her. I was jealous of her once. Now I feel pity. She was the successful one. Does she wonder how much of her success is because I left the field in which we used to compete? Then, I was patronized for the 'nice little fables' I wrote. Now, my grasp exceeds hers. She will decrease and I will increase.

"You were with Deszo." The ghost of Anna turned in my chair to face me. "Weren't you!"

"I met Deszo for coffee. We were discussing what we should do."

"About keeping your affair secret?" her apparition sneered.

"No," I sighed. "About finding a safe place for Mila."

Anna pointed at my journal and continued, "So, you feel pity for me?"

I looked at the entry. "Yes, I'm sorry that you are losing your mind."

She laughed. "That would be the only way you could surpass my achievements."

Anna picked up one of the pages she'd scattered across my desk. "You call this literature." She read one of the lines from my story, "The sharks nipped at Herkimer in their attempt to separate him from his mother. Looking back, Momma whale suddenly realized in horror, that Herkimer was gone." She tossed the page aside. "You're pathetic. I gave you my journals to edit so that you wouldn't continue to embarrass yourself and me with your insipid little stories."

I clenched my teeth and my jaws trembled with rage. "I am a writer."

"Please," Anna rolled her eyes. "You are

nothing. You married a man old enough to be your father and spent your youth playing wife. Now you are forty and a dried-up, passionless woman who stole the affections of your sister's daughter. You are a disgrace." She turned to the next page in the journal and read aloud:

> *Deszo kissed me last night. He hasn't kissed me like that since we were eighteen. We were so young then. He only had eyes for me. He said that when he looked into Anna's eyes he only saw everything I was not.*
>
> *He wanted me. I chose Max. I fell in love. I was young, Max was older and so sophisticated, I thought. Now after all these years, he still wants me. What do I want? I will always want Max. He is the only one I want. I am sorry that Anna will never know how wonderful it is to be loved as I have been loved.*

"You want him back?" Anna said. "You think I'm delusional? This nonsense you've written about Deszo is delusional. He's clearly still in love with me, not you. Never you."

"No, of course, not," I said. I watched her close the book, the shimmering image of my sister in the chair already beginning to dissipate. "Where did you go, Anna?"

Her apparition laughed and threw the book across the room. "You're my twin, where do you think I went?" Then she disappeared, wearing the dress that told me her destination.

~*~

I took Mila downstairs. Miss Szep was distressed to learn that Anna had slipped out without her knowledge. I knew she felt that she'd failed in her responsibilities as the self-appointed sentry. "It's alright," I assured her. "Anna probably went out through the back."

She agreed to let Mila spend the night. She took Mila down the hall to a small spare bedroom and told her to make herself at home. Mila put her small satchel of clothes on the floor and turned to me, "You don't have to go."

I stepped into her arms and held her close. "I'll

be back," I whispered into her hair.

I inhaled the scent of her as if I would have to remember it forever. "In the morning I'll bring you something sweet to have with your coffee."

Miss Szep took my arm and led me down the hall. She told me that if I hadn't returned by morning she would contact her friend and take Mila to Buda herself. I kissed her on both cheeks, thanked her and asked her to say a prayer for me. She smiled and said that she'd already lighted a candle to the Virgin Mary. Then I left, going down the stairs and into the cold night.

The temperature had dropped in the short time that I'd been inside. Or was it the chill that comes when fear seeps into the bones? I knew where Anna had gone. The possibility filled me with more dread than being stopped by the Nazis.

I kept to the shadows and the side streets and hurried along with my collar up, avoiding eye contact. The storefronts were shuttered, the lights of the apartments above blackened by shades or sleep. The knowledge that there would be no witness to an assault heightened my sense of vulnerability.

As I neared Deszo's building, I saw the lights were on in his apartment. I slipped in the door and crept up the stairs. At his door, I hesitated, straining to hear Anna's voice. It had been more than a year since I'd been there.

The last time was during another one of Anna's delusional episodes. At the end of their affair, she'd come to confront Deszo's wife, Katya, as being her usurper, as Anna believed she was now Deszo's wife. At that point, our phones still worked and I was called to find the two women facing off in the kitchen. Anna was raging, threatening Katya with a rolling pin. Deszo had the wretched task of facing both his wife and his mistress, neither of whom were pleased to see him.

I'd come in and talked Anna out of her hallucination, using a mixture of cajoling and promises I'd never keep. Rather than being grateful, Katya had accused me of conspiring with my sister and threatened to turn us over to the police. She knew that, at the time, Ilona and Bela were still living with us. Her threat was real.

She'd been humiliated for ten years. I sympathized with her. She'd married a man knowing that he'd not been in love with her, but married her because their families had important business ties.

I imagined that, in the beginning, she was willing to accept the bargain, hoping as all people in love do, that with time their beloved will see them differently, will return their loyalty and long-suffering with love. Like a dog waiting for a crumb from the master's table, day after day, looking with hopeful, pleading eyes.

At some point, the dog's mind turns from wanton hunger to resentment, and then fury. Not so stupid to strike out at the master, but at that which keeps its master's attention. This is what happened to Katya. Although she was the same age as Anna, her bitterness had aged her, creasing her once-lovely face with ugly furrows, and sealing shut her withered lips with unspoken venom.

She married a man in love with another woman. Not the mistress he'd later take up with, but her sister. Her twin.

~*~

We were so young then. We'd grown up together. Deszo, Anna, and I'd known each other since we were children. Our parents were friends, our fathers had been business associates, and our mothers in the same social clubs. We'd entered those frightful years of adolescence together, when childhood playmates begin to recognize the difference in their sexes.

Anna had professed her attraction to Deszo to me many nights in the bedroom we shared. I'd laughed when she'd told me that her flirtations were frustrated by the fact that he was attracted to me. "But that's impossible, we're twins. He should like you as much as he likes me!"

He didn't.

In our last year at university, I'd met Max and fallen in love. My parents threatened to disown me for loving a man who was not only twice my age, but also not Hungarian.

At first, Anna had encouraged my relationship with Max, as much as it represented rebellion and especially as it afforded her a chance to supplant my place in Deszo's heart. It hadn't.

On the night that I came home and announced to my parents that Max had asked me to marry him, Deszo was there. I remember as I walked him to the front door to say goodnight, he'd pulled me into an embrace and kissed me hard on the lips and said, "Marry me, Natalie. Not him. I love you. Marry me."

I was hurt by what I felt was his betrayal of my night of happiness. Yet, I saw in his eyes a depth of anguish that touched my heart and which I have never seen since. Not even in the eyes of my beloved husband.

Not more than six months after my marriage to Max, Deszo announced his engagement to Katya. Anna was devastated. Deszo's parents, hoping to re-direct his attention, had arranged the marriage. I remember attending his wedding, and the detached look on his face.

Anna had also attended the ceremony, and sat

next to Max and me in the church. She was unable to comprehend that Deszo had chosen another woman when he could have had her, the replica of the one he loved.

Wasn't that enough? She would love him enough for both of us.

Throughout the service she whispered to me, scathing comments about Katya's dress, about how unhappy Deszo seemed, speculated that he had been forced into the marriage. That he really did love her. That the marriage wouldn't last. I wonder if that event carried the seed of her eventual descent.

I knocked at the door. The voices stopped and then I heard footsteps in the foyer.

"It's me, Natalie," I whispered into the crack between the door and its frame.

The door's locks clicked open one by one and then I saw Deszo's face, pale and angry. I knew I was too late.

"Come in," his voice was cold. I slipped in the door and he shut it quickly behind me.

mrs. tuesday's departure

"She's been here."

"Yes," he said. "She came two hours ago. I wasn't here."

I held my breath. "Katya?"

"Yes."

"What happened?"

"Deszo?" I turned and saw Katya standing at the far end of the hall silhouetted in light. "What are you doing here?"

"It's me, Natalie," I said.

She laughed in a hideous, knowing way. "Well it couldn't be your sister."

"Where is Anna?"

"Go back to your room, Katya," he commanded.

"She should be reported too!" Katya cackled and then left us standing alone in the hallway.

"Deszo, what happened?"

He took my arm and steered me toward the living room. "Your sister came here before I got home from the café. Why weren't you at home to stop her?"

I looked at him, bewildered that he would

blame me. "She came here looking for you."

"Katya was here. They got into an argument." The exhaustion showed on his face. He crumpled into a chair and motioned me to take the chair next to him. "Anna told Katya that I was beginning an affair with you. That we'd gone out tonight to meet at the café to arrange everything."

"And Katya believed her?"

"While Anna was here, some Nazis came to the door making their random searches. This is nothing new. But this time they asked for me by name."

"Deszo, I don't understand."

He gave the words emphasis, "They told her that I was collaborating with the Allies."

"And then?"

"And then, Katya, pointed to Anna and told them that Anna had been implicated in a riot at the university the day before. That I had nothing to do with it. That Anna had come here to blackmail me."

"Oh my God," I whispered. I bent at the chest and buried my face in my hands.

"They took her."

"Where?"

"To the ghetto, to prison, I don't know."

"Can't you find out?" I jumped from my chair and stood over him. "If what Katya said is true, you must know someone!"

Deszo rose, led me to the front door, and stepped out onto the landing with me. He closed the door behind him and whispered. "Katya doesn't know anything. She suspects something because I've been gone more than usual. She's accused me of having another affair. Or, in her more hysterical moments, of collaborating with the Jews."

I grabbed the collar of his jacket, "Deszo stop lying to me. I don't care who or what you are doing. I want to find my sister."

He squeezed my hand, his grip tightened, crushing it in his own. I held back a protest of pain. His eyes met mine and he whispered, "After Katya told me what happened, I went to the police station. Anna was not there. I contacted some friends and they are going to find out where she was taken."

He released my hand and stepped back. "The best thing we can hope for is that the men who took her will be charmed by her and let her go in the morning. She must seem relatively harmless to them. They are only relying on the word of a spurned wife."

"Then why did they take her? Why not just release her? Or send her home?"

He sighed, and leaned against the wall. "Because the atmosphere in Budapest has changed."

"I have to find her. Tell me where to go."

"You can't. You'll only endanger yourself."

For the first time in my life, I wanted to slap him. "Where do these men go at night?"

A wry smile twisted Deszo's lips. "They go to places you shouldn't be seen in. Go home, go to bed. I will come to you in the morning when I have more information," he said. "Who is watching Mila while you are out?"

"A neighbor," I responded.

Deszo shook his head. "I'll take you home."

"I can't go home. I have to find Anna.

Anyway, what will Katya say if you leave with me now?"

"She won't say anything." He took my arm and steered me toward the stairs. "Let's go."

Chapter Twenty-Three

Outside, pinpricks of rain too light to see unless you looked into the dim streetlights overhead, stung my face. I huddled against Deszo's arm and watched the pavement move beneath my feet. As angry as I'd been with him, the bond was too strong to let us separate now.

We walked in silence. My mind was too shocked to notice or care which path we took down the empty streets. Where was Anna? I had no sense of dread, no echo of pain that I'd felt when she'd fallen and broken her arm when we were children. Or the bouts of confusion I'd experienced when Anna's mind had begun to turn inward and self-destruct.

We turned down a street. "Deszo, the lights in the café are still on. Remember, we saw Germans there."

The chairs were piled on the tables and Deszo had to knock at the locked doors. A woman came to the door and Deszo asked for a waitress named Mary. The woman left us and then returned. I recognized the waitress who'd waited on us earlier, standing near the door to the kitchen.

"Mary?" I asked.

He nodded. The door was unlocked and we stepped into the café. The woman looked at Mary and then taking a payment of bills returned to the kitchen.

"You shouldn't have come here now," Mary replied, looking over her shoulder.

"I wouldn't have unless it was important."

Mary looked at my face and then down the length of my body. I knew then that Anna had been here.

"I have a twin," I said. "When was she here?"

Mary didn't answer, but glanced at Deszo. He nodded and replied. "It's true. They are twins. Was her sister in here tonight?"

She took Deszo's hand, leading him away from

me. They talked in hushed voices, and she looked back at me from time to time to see if I could hear them. She was young, perhaps twenty, probably a student at the university working to support her studies, pretty, and from her body movements and the looks of approval, smitten with Deszo.

At the end of their conversation, Deszo took her hand, kissed the back of it, and then pressed some money into her palm. She turned and headed back to the kitchen, stopping once to look at me before disappearing behind the swinging doors.

Deszo came to my side and led me out the door of the café. He led me in the direction of my apartment.

"She was in there tonight, wasn't she?"

"Yes," he replied.

"Did Mary tell you who she was with? Did they leave together?"

Deszo was silent and then answered. "She came in with a group of young soldiers. They took her to a table where their senior officer was sitting. After a brief conversation, the young men left and Anna stayed with the officer."

"With no protest?"

"According to Mary, she seemed quite pleased to be there."

I shuddered. What state of mind was Anna in? What delusion could have made her stay?

"According to Mary, Anna and the German drank together until closing and then left together. They seemed very...cozy. Mary's word, not mine."

"Who did she leave with? Has he been in there before? Did she recognize him?"

Deszo nodded. "He's a frequent customer. Apparently his young men bring him girls quite regularly, or the women find him themselves."

"Why?"

Deszo laughed. "Protection. Any number of reasons to trade one favor for another."

"And he has power to grant them."

"Yes," he said. "He has the power of life and death in this situation."

"Who is he," I asked. "You seem to know him."

"I know of him," Deszo said. "Do you remember the German sitting at the table next to ours? The one who asked you to join him?"

I shivered, recalling my reluctant physical attraction to him. His eyes drew you in, the way he looked at you as if he already knew what you were feeling. "Yes."

"That's the one Anna was with."

No. No, I thought. Could Anna have discovered that this man thought she was me? With that knowledge, what had she done?

"Where did they go?" I asked. "Did Mary tell you?"

Deszo lead me up the front steps of my building. "She doesn't know where they went. She said that Anna went willingly, happily."

"Is there any way we can find out?"

"Not tonight," Deszo held the door for me.

The stairwell was dark and silent. Deszo allowed me to take his arm but his body was stiff, his thoughts far away. I imagined this must be uncomfortable for him, even though he'd broken up with Anna a year ago.

"I'll make more inquiries in the morning and find out where she's been taken."

"Thank you," I whispered.

As we passed the door to Miss Szep's apartment, I stopped.

"Mila's there. I should bring her upstairs, shouldn't I?"

I rapped lightly on the front door. There was no answer. I knocked again, harder this time.

"Who is it?"

"Miss Szep, it's Natalie."

The bolts were drawn back, the door unlocked and opened. Miss Szep stood peering out into the hall, squinting. "Is something wrong? Did you find Anna?"

"No," I said. "We know who Anna left with, but we don't know where she is. Can I get Mila?"

Miss Szep hesitated, "She's sleeping."

"I'm glad to hear that, but I'd really like her to come upstairs with me."

"I will still take her to my friend's house tomorrow?"

"Yes," I agreed. "I think that's best. Until things are settled with Anna, it will be safer for Mila if she's not here."

"I'll come upstairs in the morning," Miss Szep said, clearly reciting plans she'd determined not to change. "Mila and I will go to Miss Gödel's house. I will stay there with Mila until you can come to join her."

"That's too much for you!" I said. "Who will take care of your cat?"

Miss Szep chuckled. "Nero will come with us. Miss Gödel's cat, Horatio, will enjoy the company. We'll be fine, don't worry."

Then she closed the door and I heard her footsteps retreating down the hall. A few minutes later Mila appeared at the door clutching her belongings, yawning under the lingering spell of sleep. "Nana! Did you find Anna?"

I put my arm around her shoulders and nodded to Miss Szep. "We'll see you in the morning."

I led Mila up the stairs. Deszo followed us, taking the key from my hand at the top of the stairs, and unlocking the door and holding it open for us. "Mila, we are very close to finding Anna," he said as she passed. "Don't worry; we believe she is safe for the night."

~*~

Our eyes met and I smiled in gratitude for his encouraging words.

I guided Mila down the hall to her room. At the entrance, she stopped and turned to me. "Can I sleep in your bed tonight, Nana?"

I hugged her and turned back toward my bedroom. "Of course, I would like that very much."

She turned down the duvet on my bed and then looked back at me. "You don't think I'm being childish."

"I will be very lonely for the few days that we are separated." I smiled and walked to the bed and pulled the covers over her as she slid over to the far side of the bed I once shared with Max. "I'm glad you thought of it. It's like a slumber party."

Mila snuggled beneath the cover and made a nest of the down-filled pillow. I stood for a moment just admiring the way her dark hair arrayed against the white pillow casing and caught the light.

She was so young and so beautiful. I wish she'd grown up in my time, in the loving, peaceful home I'd known. My heart ached with the knowledge of what she'd seen in her young life.

Chapter Twenty-Four

"Nana?" Mila called to me from beneath the duvet. "Anna said that you've begun writing again. Are you working on a new story?"

I managed a weak smile and then sat on the edge of the bed and began gently rubbing Mila's back. "Yes, I've started a new project. It's a story just for you."

"What's it about?" Mila asked excitedly. "Am I in it?"

"Yes, my sweet, you are." I tilted my head and looked into Mila's eyes. "And you are on an exciting adventure to America."

Mila's eyes widened. "America? Oh, that sounds wonderful. But how do I get there?"

I thought back to my story. "How about on a beautifully decorated hot air balloon with a basket big enough to hold a bed and a chair and a little table so your journey would be comfortable?"

"I like that. But, how about a balloon big enough to carry a cottage, so that you could come, too? It would be so quiet and lovely to float among the clouds. And I would need a telescope so that I could watch for whales as I cross the ocean and then look for land. You would come with me, wouldn't you?"

"I'll be sure that the balloon is big enough to carry a little cottage, big enough for me and you."

"Oh Nana, I wish it were true."

"I'll make it true, somehow," I whispered as I rose from the bed and walked to the door. I shut off the light and paused before closing the door, "Good night, my sweet Mila."

"Good night, Nana."

Deszo was waiting for me in my study. He'd made coffee and was standing at the window looking out onto the street when I came in.

"She should be asleep soon, I hope." I poured a cup of coffee and went to join him by the window.

"It looks peaceful out there at this hour," he

said as I moved to his side.

"I used to love the hours after midnight, the quiet, the solitude, being inside safe to watch and not be harmed."

"Now it's not safe to be inside," he said.

What I'd learned about him tonight had changed the history of which I was certain. He had become another man. Still the same, but a door had opened onto a new corridor I wasn't sure I wanted to travel. Should I trust him?

"I think Anna will be fine tonight."

"Tonight, but not tomorrow?"

He shrugged. "In the morning everyone looks different. We wake up and remember who we are, not who we imagined we were the night before."

"Do you think she will come home in the morning?"

"If she can," he said and took a final sip from his coffee and then put down the cup. "I should go home now. I'll come tomorrow after I've made some inquiries."

I followed him to the front door. So many unanswered questions were left. The lines of exhaustion that drew dark circles under his eyes stopped me. His mind already far away, working on the problem that faced him and many others I knew nothing about.

He opened the front door and stepped out onto the landing. He took me in his arms and drew me closer. "Natalie," he paused and kissed my forehead, lingering for a moment. "Do you remember how easy it was for us?"

I bowed my head. "Yes."

His fingers ran from my scalp to the edges of my hair where they stopped and grasped the ends at the nape of my neck. I leaned against his coat and inhaled his scent, my arms went around him and I wanted to stay there, feeling the same security I once felt at my post by the window, safe inside. I listened to the rhythm of his breathing until it matched my own.

"There will be an end to this madness. There are people working to make that happen." He pulled away from me and descended the stairs without looking back.

I closed the door and walked down the hall.

My footsteps echoed in the stillness. I hoped he was right, though I felt that for Budapest, the end would not come before a torrent was unleashed.

After hanging my clothes in the closet and putting my robe on over my nightgown, I went to the bathroom, but there was no hot water for a bath. I turned and saw my face in the mirror over the sink. I leaned over, turned on the tap, washed the remnants of makeup off my face, and then brushed my teeth.

I walked past my room pausing to check on Mila. The gentle breath of Mila's sleep was a comfort. It would be lovely to hold her in my arms, the daughter I'd always wished for. I closed my eyes and prayed that this would not be good-bye, but only a safe passage to the other side of the nightmare. I wanted to feel her solidity next to me, the way she curled in a ball against my back when she was a child and had climbed in my bed in the middle of the night when her mother had not come home.

I stopped at the threshold of Anna's room; its emptiness rebuked me with the truth of her accusations earlier in the evening.

"We've grown so far apart haven't we?" I whispered.

"But it wasn't always that way was it, Natalie?" Her voice came from somewhere near her vanity. I smiled. Of course it would.

"You've always been vain, Anna."

"Do you remember when we were six and Momma entered us in that beauty pageant?" Anna's apparition was sitting on the bench in front of the vanity. She leaned back, looking at me as she brushed her hair.

I thought about it, trying to recall the memory, and then shook my head.

"Well I do."

"Why? What was so special about that day?"

"You were scared to walk up on the stage!" Anna put down her brush and got up, walked over to me and took my hand. "But I wasn't. So I told you I would be brave for both of us."

Her hand had the substance of a warm breath, but it was enough on this lonely night. I sighed, finally remembering the event from our childhood.

"Yes. You held my hand and just before we walked on the stage you kissed me on the cheek and told me that I was the most beautiful girl there."

"You were!"

"It was only years later that I realized you were complimenting yourself as much as me!"

Anna giggled, "But it worked!"

"Momma was so proud when we won the blue ribbon." I leaned over and kissed the air where I saw the faint shimmer of her cheek. I hoped my kiss would bring her as much courage tonight as hers had then.

I thought of her with the German I'd met at the café the night before and wondered where they'd gone. I hoped that she was safe. She was my other half. Without her, a part of me was lost, drifting out to sea, listing to the side as her mind descended into madness. I feared what would happen if she capsized.

"Anna, come back to me. Or I will come to you."

The darkness was dappled with shadows as my eyes adjusted. Anna's curtains stood open, the windows covered only by white lace sheers that let the light come in filtered so that beams of light struggled, strong and weak, fighting to claim dominance over the dark. Failing, but beautiful in their sacrifice.

My toes were ghostly white and speckled in the magical shallows. The boom of a cannon and the answer of machine gun fire shook me, but did not move me from the spot. I was captured by the ordinariness of my feet and the laws of physics that defied mandates of madmen, which allowed light to shine in the darkness.

Chapter Twenty-Five

The knock came at six a.m. I'd held Mila through the night, unable to sleep, resting in the meditation of her breaths. How many times had I kissed her brow during the few hours between climbing into bed and this signal that intruded upon our dreams? Mila stirred and turned away from me.

In the dawn's silence, I lifted the covers and slipped from the bed. The hall seemed longer as I walked toward the door. How quickly the time had come for me to release Mila to someone else. Just for a short while, and then I would join her. It was for the best.

I passed the old paintings that lined the hall, my fingers running along the base of their frames conjuring up flashes of memories from my childhood, my marriage.

Each step I took quickened my progress like Alice in Wonderland sliding down the rabbit's hole, grasping for branches to slow her fall into the inevitable.

When I opened the door, the events would be set in motion. What if I didn't open the door?

I stopped. My hand lingered on the lock. I heard Miss Szep's urgent whispers on the other side. "Natalie, it's me."

Of course. Who else would it be? The Nazis? Perhaps. If, Mrs. Nyugati had her way. We had so many enemies these days. Who knew what they looked like? The best disguise was the friend.

I longed to turn away from the door. To go to the kitchen and make breakfast for Mila and surprise her just as she'd surprised me the other morning, bringing breakfast to her in bed.

We could share coffee and toast and talk about where we'd go later in the day. I wanted to take her to the little store where I bought my pens and paper. It was time that she'd started her own journal. I wanted to instruct her in the ways of a writer. She had the talent, the curiosity, and enough experience to fill the blank pages with words that would wrestle her innocence against reality.

The cold steel of the lock was slippery beneath my fingers, but it released its hold on the door. Automatic actions, done more quickly because our subconscious intuition tells us that hesitation will complicate matters. Perhaps that is what made it easier for the enemy to accomplish their atrocities. The instinctual trust of the victims made their destruction effortless.

Miss Szep hurried past me. "Is Mila ready to go? I think it will be better if we have an early start."

I took her to the kitchen, offered her a seat at the table and put on water for the coffee. "Mila is still sleeping, but I'll go and wake her and get her ready. Can you manage the coffee? We have bread over there."

~*~

When the door closed behind them, I stood listening to their footsteps echo down the stairs, holding onto the sound as if it too was a remnant that I could embrace in Mila's absence. I stood at my door long after the sound of the front door closing downstairs signaled their departure onto the street. I stood there hoping they'd turn around and come back. I stood there because I didn't know what else to do.

I was lost in the enormity of my loneliness. Snippets of conversations between my mother and father rang in my ears. The squeal of our young voices, Anna and I, running through the house playing a game of hide and seek with our baby sister Ilona.

My father choking on a puff from his pipe the first time he met Max and realized just how much older my husband would be. The laughter later, when Max brought out his own pipe after dinner and joined my father in a discussion among sweet-smelling smoke and deals made between fathers and their daughter's suitors.

I went to my room and climbed into bed. I

crawled over to the side of the bed where Mila had slept and clutched her pillow to my face inhaling the faint smell of her.

Finally, I wept, the sobs wracking my body.

Chapter Twenty-Six

What was that rapping sound? A woodpecker? Max and I were having a picnic in a meadow. We sat under the shady arms of a weeping willow tree on a red plaid blanket I'd taken from the closet in the hall. The wicker basket was emptied of its contents.

So peaceful, only the song of birds overshadowed the sound of the breeze in the branches above. It was warm, Max was wearing his tan linen suit, and he'd taken off his jacket and rolled up the sleeves of his soft blue shirt.

I was wearing a cotton dress with a full skirt. It had a white background with a pattern of bright red cherries that matched the red buttons that ran up the front of the dress.

I wore my hair pulled back from my face, the

way Max liked it, and tied with a scarf. I'd taken off my shoes and stockings so I could enjoy the feel of the grass and the warm sun against my skin.

Max raised a glass of champagne and toasted our anniversary. "You are more beautiful now," he said.

"I am so tired."

"Still beautiful."

"Not anymore."

He took a sliver of cheese and held it up to my lips. I took it into my mouth and held it until it melted against my tongue and I swallowed its buttery, acid tang. His fingers rested against my cheek and then traced a line down my neck, following the lines to my collarbone and down over my breast.

"I'm sorry that we never had children," he said. "You are a wonderful mother."

"Mila is an ideal child," I said leaning my head against his chest. "I wish she were ours."

"She is yours, isn't she?"

"I am her caretaker, but her heart still belongs to Ilona."

"But she loves you," he said.

"Of course, but not the way she loves her mother. Strange, we always long for the one who doesn't love us. Like Anna and Deszo."

"Or are incapable of loving us, like Deszo and you."

I picked up one of the figs I'd cut and lifted it to his lips. His bite spilled its juice onto my fingers.

"You left me too soon," I said finishing the sweet remnant he'd left. "This would be so much easier if you were here."

Max nodded and then took my hand in his. "You are becoming a woman I never saw. I expected you were loyal, but I see that you are also very brave. I am so proud of you."

I raised his hand to my lips and kissed the soft furrow of skin between his knuckles.

"I hope you won't waste your life waiting for these moments."

"But they're all I have!"

"Dreams?" Max shook his head. "I would never have asked that of you."

"They are enough."

"No," he sighed. "Dreams are not meant to supplant life."

"I don't want you to leave me, not ever."

Max kissed me in a soft lingering kiss, the pressure of his lips against mine warmed me and my body ached in return. He lifted his head and looked into my eyes. "Deszo is a good man."

"I'm not so sure anymore."

"He loves you."

"I don't love him." I pushed myself up and brushed the crumbs off my lap. "You are all I want."

"Before me, you loved Deszo," Max said, running his hand down my spine. "I was an interruption. A detour."

"No!" I pulled away and buried my face in my hands. "You are the only one I wanted."

"Now it's time to move on," Max whispered.

"No! I won't!"

"I will always be with you, Natalie." He moved to my side and took me in his arms, leaning me back against his body. He nuzzled his face against my neck and kissed me again. "Our love will never be diminished, but will you spend the rest of your life like Anna, pining for a love that has gone?"

"It's not the same! You were taken from me, Deszo never loved Anna."

"True, but you both wish for something you can't have. Neither one of you is willing to let go of the past."

"But I have Mila now." I watched five sparrows dive and swoop heavenward again.

"For how long?" Max replied stroking my hair. "And is giving your love to her, while she waits for her mother to return, enough?"

"Will it turn out badly, Max?" I asked, putting his hand in my lap.

His fingers stretched against my thigh and warmed my skin. His eyes drank in my face and he smiled and then looked away.

The woodpecker above our head rattled against the tree again. I awoke.

The knock at the door was insistent. I threw the covers I'd wrapped around me to the side and stumbled out of bed. The room was filled with light and I knew that hours had passed since I had lain down. I threw my robe around my shoulders and went to the front door hoping to find Anna on the other side.

I opened the door and saw Jozef. "What are you doing here?"

He walked around me and I closed the door, following him into the kitchen. He sat down at the table and motioned me to join him.

I repeated my question, as I took a seat across from him. "What are you doing here?"

"I saw Mila and your neighbor leave this morning," he said. "So I followed them. I know where they are staying. So far, they are safe."

I ignored the implication of blackmail made possible by his knowledge. Alternatively, the real question of why he'd been outside our building at such an early hour. "Were there any problems for them? What's the place like?"

Jozef got up from the table and rinsed out the cups that were left from earlier. He filled the kettle with water and prepared a new pot of coffee. "Actually your idea was perfect," he said.

"It wasn't mine."

He looked at me and raised his eyebrows. "You are trusting. Have you known the old woman for very long?"

"Yes, my parents knew her. She's been my neighbor since I was a child."

"Well, Mila and the old woman looked like grandmother and granddaughter. They're staying in a small house, with a fenced yard and enough shrubs to hide it from the eyes of someone walking by. The neighbors' houses are similar, so I'm guessing that they keep to themselves. Although they'd know if someone new had entered the street."

"Miss Szep has known the woman they're staying with for years. So her visit shouldn't be cause for alarm," I countered.

"Your sister and you will join them?"

I hesitated. Jozef stepped into the hall, "Hello?"

He came back into the kitchen and went to the stove to check the kettle. "Your sister has gone-missing, or is she visiting a friend too?"

I didn't answer.

"Where was she last seen?"

"At the café, last night."

There was a knock. I went to the front door and heard Deszo's voice. I looked back to see Jozef standing in the hall. I opened the door and Deszo entered. His face was pale and haggard from lack of sleep. "They've taken Mila."

"No! You're wrong; Jozef said that they were all right. He said they had gotten to the house safely!"

Deszo spoke to Jozef as if they'd met before. "What are you doing here?"

"You know each other?" In our last conversation, Jozef behaved as if he knew of Deszo, not that he'd met him. "What is going on here? Tell me!"

"They must have taken her after I left," Jozef said.

"Or did you tell them where she was?" Deszo's face contorted with fury. "How much did you get for the capture?"

"They want Natalie," Jozef said, nodding at

Deszo. "And you. Not Mila or Anna."

"What do they want with us?"

"I don't know why they want you," Jozef hesitated and then continued. "But they want to make a deal with Deszo."

"Why did they take them?" I asked.

"Incentive," Deszo replied.

"Where are they being held? Can I see them? Are they hurt?"

"I don't know where they're holding them, but they told me that they will be taken care of."

"What if I don't go to the meeting?" Deszo leaned against the wall and folded his arms across his chest. His face changed, gone was the anger, and in its place was a placid look of disinterest.

"Deszo, you must," I urged. "Or I will go alone."

"They will be sent to the camps."

I felt the floor move beneath my feet like quicksand. I reached out and grasped Deszo's arm to keep from falling. "Deszo," I whispered. "They won't survive the camps."

Deszo pulled me into his arms and held me

tightly. "When is the meeting?"

"Tonight, I'll give you directions," Jozef replied. "We'll meet together beforehand, and I will take you there."

"What is your reward for this arrangement," Deszo hissed. "I imagine the prize is quite large."

Jozef's jaw worked, bunching the muscles in his face. "I work for both sides. The information I get from the Germans I supply to certain groups who are trying to save the Jews."

"Do they pay as well as the Germans?"

Jozef waved away the question. "Sometimes they pay better. And with them, I can sleep at night."

"How well will you sleep tonight?"

Jozef stared at Deszo and responded, "I'm going to speak with one of them before I pick you up. I'll try to find out where they are holding Mila and Anna, and if there is any way to smuggle them out if things don't go well tonight."

Chapter Twenty-Seven

Deszo held my hand and led me along the narrow steps that climbed up the back of the old hotel. The lights in the building were shut off during an earlier air raid and had yet to come back on.

"Why didn't Jozef show up?" I whispered to the dark shape of Deszo's back. We had waited nearly thirty minutes for his arrival at a designated location one block from the hotel.

We waited, following every shadow that crossed the path of the alley we stood in. Each time, the hollow echo of footsteps carried away the hope of his arrival. He told us the location of the meeting in the event that he was unable to come. However, he had not told us who would be there, only that they were high-ranking officers who were willing to negotiate an exchange.

Deszo didn't answer my question, because there were only two possibilities. Either Jozef had been detained and was probably now in danger himself, or he had served us up like Judas. Both weakened our position, the latter would be fatal.

The stairs were old, iron-waffled steps hung against the wall by rusting bolts that shuddered under the weight of our every footfall. What once allowed the hotel staff to scurry between floors undetected, had been abandoned to rot.

I imagined Jozef flying up these steps on his errands of so-called business with the enemy. Betrayer or savior, I imagined he was capable of either if the price was right. I believed he chose who to protect and who to sell according to an internal compass that had nothing to do with politics or money, but some idiosyncratic logic that only he understood.

The Germans had chosen this rendezvous wisely. It was an old, private hotel, small enough so that they could capture, police, and inhabit all of its rooms easily. In my mother's day, it was a place where the literati met artists from Paris or London or Moscow. The lobby had been well appointed in those days, a small bar off the lobby provided a

discreet meeting place for adoring women to meet a 'friend' before retreating upstairs.

At the third landing, Deszo stopped in front of a closed door.

"This is it," he said.

"Should we wait?"

"We're late already." Deszo slowly opened the door, revealing more darkness.

"Are you sure this is the right floor?"

He took my hand and we slipped through the doorway. Our footsteps were muffled on the carpet that ran down the length of the hall.

There was no sound coming from the closed doors that lined either side of the hall. The heat had been turned off ages ago and the temperature felt even colder than the outside air.

Deszo stopped in front of a set of double doors at the end, leading to what I guessed would be a suite. He rapped lightly and waited.

After a moment, we heard steps approaching

the door on the other side. A man's voice asked us our business in German. Deszo responded in kind saying that we were expected.

The footsteps retreated and then returned and the door was unlocked. The person who opened it stood behind the door, in the shadows, so that we were unable to see his face. He gestured us ahead and then followed as we walked down a short foyer that lead into the living room of the suite.

We stopped on the threshold. I held my breath wondering if this was what hell would look like.

Pools of light from ancient candelabras cast irregular shadows around the room. The candelabras were placed haphazardly on a desk, a grand piano, a bar, and the side tables on either end of the couch that sat in the center of the room facing us. Heavy velvet curtains covered the windows and cascaded in bloody pools on the floor. The room was oppressively warm and smoke-filled from cigarettes, and the remnants of a fire in the fireplace. Still, I shivered.

The air stank of the sweet musk of sweat that comes from fear and torture, from those receiving and inflicting. In a corner of the room, a broken chair lay on its side, wounded in some battle, its frame scavenged to feed the fire.

"Welcome." The words came not from the sullen German who sat on the couch observing us with disdain as he cleaned his gun. I turned and swallowed the breath that threatened to escape from my mouth in a whimper.

Deszo stepped in front of me. "Our escort never showed up."

The German shrugged and gestured toward one of the three closed doors that stood like sentries on either side of the living room.

"The two on the left are currently occupied. We'll go to my room." He gestured to the single door on the right, which I guessed led to the master bedroom. I looked back at the other two doors and wondered who or what was held behind them. The other soldiers had managed a brief, knowing smile at his comment.

As he stepped out of the shadows, I gasped. He smiled at my recognition. Taking my hand in his, he bowed over it and raised it to his lips, kissing the back as he held it firmly in his grasp.

He straightened up, but did not release his grip. "It's good to see you again."

"You were in the café," I said, pulling my hand away. He was more handsome than I remembered. He was wearing cologne that was familiar, I recalled the man who'd passed me on the street, after I'd left the café. He'd been wearing the same scent. It had reminded me of Max. I felt its impact in the small of my center, like hot melting wax. Gunter.

"That was the first time." He reached for my elbow and escorted me toward the door to his room. The wool of his jacket rubbed against my breast as he led me. The scent of him surrounded me now. I saw the lightest shadow of blonde growth on his chin. "The second occasion was on the road. You were walking with your young friend."

"You were in the car?"

He cocked his head to the side, and offered the proof I didn't need to hear. "My assistant spoke to Jozef. I was sitting on the other side of the car. I doubt you could see me from where you were standing."

I thought back to that evening. I'd been so frightened that I could barely recall the face of the German that Jozef had spoken to. I remembered he had consulted with someone else sitting next to him. I'd never considered how unlikely it was that we'd been let go so easily.

Gunter stopped at the closed door and released my arm. "You were lucky that I was in that car. Your evening might have turned out much worse if I weren't."

He leaned toward the door and opened it, stepping aside so that Deszo and I could enter first, and he could observe our reaction.

The room was as large as the living room, but as opulent and neat whereas the other room had been disheveled.

Tears of anger pricked the edges of my eyes as I entered the room of the trespasser.

Against the far wall a large bed sat on a pedestal, its frame draped with an overstuffed duvet most likely stolen from a rich man's home.

Beside the windowed doors leading to a small balcony overlooking the street, were two chairs covered in maroon damask silk.

Gunter lead us to a long, narrow table covered in starched, white linen with three place settings of fine china arranged around one end, and a bottle of red wine decanting. The centerpiece was a candelabrum holding new tapers. The light danced under a breeze coming from some unknown source.

"If you don't mind, I'll sit at the head of the table," he said moving to a tall ornately carved mahogany chair. "Please join me. Natalie, sit on my right. Professor Eckhart, you will take the seat on my left."

I hesitated, waiting to take my cue from Deszo. He didn't acknowledge my gaze but took the seat he'd been offered. Gunter held my chair and both men waited until I was seated.

Chapter Twenty-Eight

"Let's begin." Deszo placed his hands on either side of his plate. "You want information from me and we want Natalie's sister and niece."

Gunter ignored Deszo's attempt to lead the conversation. Instead, the German picked up a small silver bell next to his plate and rang it. Instantly, a young soldier appeared carrying a large tray holding three covered serving dishes. He set them on the table and the soldier stood back, waiting. Gunter waved him away and the soldier departed as wordlessly as he'd entered.

Gunter lifted the silver, domed lids from each plate with a flourish. "I hope I've chosen dishes you'll enjoy."

Anger rose in my throat as I gazed longingly at meats and vegetables I hadn't seen or been able to purchase at any price in the past year. Saliva filled my mouth at the memory of their taste. The injustice of the meal and its circumstances twisted my stomach and sent a shiver traveling the length of my spine.

What fine cuisine awaited Anna and Mila tonight? When was the last time they'd eaten? Perhaps that was the point of Gunter's gesture, to show that he could provide what others could not.

"Excuse my manners," Gunter picked up one of the dishes and deftly placed a thick slab of roast meat on my plate. "You don't have a problem with pork do you?"

I ignored his reference and reluctantly savored the smell. I was so hungry. My hands remained in my lap. He offered the plate to Deszo and then repeated the motion with the other two dishes.

I looked to Deszo for guidance. His silence bothered me. Why hadn't he raised an objection to this grotesque charade? How could he sit here as comfortably as if he were dining with colleagues from the university? He smiled at me, looking relaxed and enjoying the prospect of a well-cooked meal at the end of a hard day. All of the apprehension he'd shown when we were waiting in the alley was gone.

"Forgive me, you're Catholic aren't you?" Gunter said to me. "Perhaps you'd like to pray before we eat."

I nodded and crossed myself. I prayed silently.

"Ah, to be a mind reader," Gunter sighed, picking up his fork.

I thought of the book of *Genesis*. There are two versions of Eve's meeting with the serpent. I contemplated the disguises of the devil as I considered Gunter's handsome, though hardly benign face.

"I understand you are a widow." He took my hand in his and clasped it as if in understanding. His skin was warm and surprisingly smooth. In other circumstances, I might be his lover. Were we really so different? He was a man. I was a woman. Had this not been war, he would simply be a German, perhaps a businessman in town to close a deal. Maybe we had things in common, a love of literature, or music. We would go to Buda to visit the old castle. We would dine together after seeing a performance of *La Boehme* at the Opera.

"I never married," he sighed. "You must find it difficult to be alone at a time like this?"

His tone surprised me, so comforting. "Yes," I said.

His eyes were a translucent green, like the warm, shallow waters of the ocean Max and I had visited on our honeymoon on the French coast. Perhaps he was a reluctant participant in this war. Certainly, such an un-furrowed brow could not have worried over atrocities. He must have found a way to avoid being a party to them. It was late in the war, everyone said that. He'd not been a party to the worst. He'd been drafted late, not willingly of course.

"You're not eating."

Dutifully, I picked up my fork, cut a piece and raised the succulent meat to my lips.

"That's better," he smiled, reaching for the bottle. "Will you join me in a glass of wine?"

"Professor." Gunter filled our glasses and turned his attention to Deszo. "I understand that you have many friends in the higher ranks of our army."

"I have friends in many areas of society." Deszo put down his knife and fork, raised his glass to his lips, and took a long sip.

"Those connections do not concern me. I'm interested in who you are talking to within my army, and why." Gunter picked up the bell and rang it. The young soldier who'd brought in our dinner now appeared carrying another tray. He set the tray down cleared our dishes and set out cups of coffee, brandy glasses and a decanter. He served us quickly and departed.

Gunter picked up the glass of brandy and swirled the contents. He held the glass up to the candlelight and studied the amber liquid. "Connections are important." He spoke slowly, carefully. "It's amazing what you can accomplish when you know the right people. Or what you can obtain. Take this brandy, for example. I received a case of it as a present from a grateful man. Why?" He shrugged. "Gratitude."

Deszo scanned the room, "You must have a lot

of people who are grateful to you."

Gunter brought the glass to his lips, took a long sip, held it in his mouth moving the liquid slowly around before swallowing it. "It lives up to its reputation." He put the glass down and looked at Deszo as if just recognizing his comment. "You'd be amazed by how many friends I've made since coming to your city. I'd heard such nasty rumors about how uncivilized the Hungarians are, but they must be referring to the villagers. They were not so hospitable to us."

I cringed, remembering the stories that had reached the city detailing the massacres the Germans had wrought against the villagers who'd tried to defend themselves.

Gunter continued, as if talking to himself, "But the citizens of Budapest. Very nice people."

Since his first sip of brandy he had withdrawn into himself, his questions to Deszo off-hand, his remarks slow in coming as if it were an effort to process Deszo's words, though both men spoke in German.

The candles were burning low. Their life

hurried by a mysterious breeze that caused them to dance too quickly.

"It's a welcome relief to meet cultured people. Fine food tastes better when shared with those sophisticated enough to appreciate what they are being provided."

Deszo steepled his fingers and looked at a spot somewhere on the wall behind me. "I'm sure a poor, hungry man would appreciate this meal as much as a cultured one."

"That's not the point, is it?" Gunter's brow creased in disapproval. "Clearly, one's more worthy than the other."

"My sister would have enjoyed this meal as much as I did," I whispered.

Gunter sighed as if explaining the most rudimentary principal to a thickheaded child. "Natalie, of course, there are exceptions."

"I'm sure you understand the distinction, Professor."

"Please, call me Deszo."

Gunter re-filled his glass and once again went through the process of swirling the brandy and holding it up to the candlelight. He raised it to his nose, inhaled deeply, put his head back against the chair, and closed his eyes.

Deszo was again staring at the spot behind my head. We sat in a collective silence of a minute, then two, and then I heard Gunter's voice, "Sometimes I understand that his mission has the best intentions. He's really just trying to create a better world. Isn't that admirable?"

I shivered.

"It's a shame that it has to be so messy. If the English weren't so damned determined to hold onto Palestine, we could have simply shipped them out of the country rather than…well, rather than the other way."

"You mean the camps," Deszo matched his tone to Gunter's.

Gunter ran his hand over his closed eyes. "Those camps are a nuisance; our military personnel would be better utilized in the field. You can't imagine what a logistical nightmare it is to move so many people. You've got to wonder why the Allies haven't bombed the railways we use to herd the cattle." He laughed, "That's an allusion, Professor. You know we use cattle cars, don't you? Not as comfortable as passenger cars, but more efficient.

The meal we'd just enjoyed curdled in my stomach. The flickering candlelight exposed raised, white scar tissue cutting across Gunter's neck. I wondered whether it was self-inflicted or a remnant of battle.

His breathing deepened and he hummed a snippet of a waltz. He had no more than a glass of wine with his dinner, so it was unlikely that he was drunk.

Deszo took a sip of his brandy and pulled a packet of cigarettes out of his coat pocket. He slipped one into his mouth, lighted it and took a long puff, exhaling a long stream of smoke over the candelabra.

He watched the direction of the smoke change as it hit the current of air coming from the hidden source behind me. He examined the glowing ash and then absently tapped it on the edge of his saucer.

"What do you talk to my officers about?" Gunter asked from behind his closed eyes. "Are you a spy? Or more interestingly, are you working for us?"

Deszo continued to smoke as if he hadn't heard the question.

"Of course, you wouldn't tell me either way," Gunter smiled. "That wouldn't be fun, would it?"

Deszo leaned back in his chair and with a thrust of his jaw blew out one, two, three rings of smoke, following their progress with his eyes.

"You know your friend Jozef works both sides of the street," Gunter continued, seemingly taking no notice of Deszo's silence.

"He fancies himself a clever little businessman. He has been quite useful to us in gathering information. His prices are reasonable, but I don't understand his motives. At least not in this case. He's quite loyal to Natalie, and to the young one, Mila, I believe she's called? At first, I thought he was related or, at the very least, well paid by Natalie. But after extensive conversation…" Gunter laughed, sat up and examined his fingernails. "Yes, quite extensive. He still claims that he hasn't been paid at all."

Deszo held out his packet of cigarettes to Gunter, who took one and then Deszo's cigarette to light his own.

After he'd exhaled a plume of smoke, Gunter continued. "He's here by the way."

"Where?"

Gunter ignored my question and turned to Deszo. "Do you convey information to the Swedes? That idiot Wallenberg, I'm sure you've come across him in your travels. He hides behind the shield of the Consulate and prints up false papers to save the Jews. Do you know he worked for a Jew during his younger days in business? He's probably being paid by them. You don't actually think the Swedish are so altruistic that they are issuing passports for free?"

"I believe they are as appalled by your slaughter of Jews as other countries." Deszo crushed the butt of his cigarette on the rim of the fine china. I noticed that Gunter visibly winced as if he had felt the last burning embers. Gunter recovered quickly, dropped his cigarette to the floor, and slowly ground it under the heel of his boot.

"Do you really think that the Allies don't know what goes on in our camps? They don't discuss it in the newspapers, but they know. Their planes carry cameras as well as bombs.

"They make insignificant gestures using men like yourself or Wallenberg so that when this is all over they can save face. We know the truth, don't we? They're only slightly bothered that we are ridding the world of Jews.

"But I'm curious about your motivations, Deszo," Gunter continued. "You don't appear to be a man in need of the spotlight. It would be much easier, no doubt safer, for you to sit on the sidelines. We both know at this point that the war is nearly over. I've checked your background. You have no Jewish blood running through your veins. The mistress you cast aside is out of the way and you've got her lovely and sane twin sitting next to you."

Deszo took a sip of his brandy and then spoke

over the rim of the glass. "Your research is admirable, but like your theories about the Allies, lacking in interpretation. I'm not here to talk about that. I'm here to negotiate with you— information in exchange for Anna and Mila."

Gunter shoved himself back from the table and stood. "You are not in charge!"

Deszo continued taking no notice of Gunter's rising temper. "And now you want to spend the evening discussing politics. Well, I am pleased to join you another evening for such a conversation. But not while these two innocent women are sitting in a ghetto."

Gunter began pacing. "I give you the finest wine and brandy to be found in this God-forsaken city," his fists punched the air. "I feed you food you haven't tasted in years. You are so impatient! Do you want to see your messenger boy. He's here!"

"Where?"

Gunter turned, his eyes narrowed and his lips formed a thin smile. "You see, this is what I don't understand. Your interest in the boy. He's a thief, you know."

Deszo shot me a warning glance. "She has a soft spot for him because he's close in age to Mila."

"I think there must be more to it than that, eh Natalie?"

Both men had become enigmas. Deszo downplayed our relationship to Jozef, but at what expense? Jozef's safety? I shook my head and looked down at the table.

"Perhaps Natalie should leave now," Deszo said. "One of your men could escort her home. Safely."

"Again, you are trying to direct things," Gunter sighed. "No, Natalie is going to stay. She reminds me of her sister. Whose company I enjoyed very much, last night."

"What did you do with my sister?" I demanded. I tried to stand, but Deszo grabbed my arm and pushed me back down in my seat.

"Silence," he hissed. "Don't say another word about Anna."

"That would be a good idea," Gunter agreed. "You might not like what you hear, my dear. But I can assure you, from our short time together this evening, you two are nothing alike. And oddly, your sister seems to be much less concerned with your welfare."

"Why Anna? From what I saw at the café, you have plenty of beautiful women at your disposal," Deszo countered.

Gunter waved away his comment and walked to the windows on the other side of the room.

Chapter Twenty-Nine

"What will you offer in exchange for the sister and the young girl?" Gunter ran his hand along the back of one of the chairs, and pulled the drapes to one side. "Tell me how valuable are these women to you, Deszo?"

"You overestimate the information I have access to," Deszo said, not turning to face Gunter.

"Mila is not too young to be of service to me or my men," Gunter said.

"She's a child!" I gasped.

"She wouldn't be the first," Gunter replied as he continued to stare into the black night.

Deszo put up his hand to silence my reply. This was insane. I thought of Mila and realized I would rather she die than face the torture of being used by these men. "Tell me what I can offer you,"

I said. "I will take Mila's place."

"Natalie," Deszo warned. "Don't."

"But not your sister's?" Gunter turned from the curtain and gazed across the room at me. "Not your twin?"

"Mila is a child."

Gunter ignored my response and turned toward Deszo. "You're right, she has no place in these discussions. But I always enjoy the sound of a pleading woman."

"Then send her home, now."

Gunter considered the request. "Do you want to go home, Natalie?"

"Not without Mila and Anna."

He smiled grimly and then shook his head. "Then you will have to stay a little longer."

"Where are they now?"

Gunter stared out the window and sighed. "They are with others."

"Are they together?" I asked.

He seemed to consider this question and then turned to me, "I don't think so. Although, anything is possible."

"What do you mean by this? Are they all right? Are they still alive?"

He picked up a heavy marble ashtray that sat on the small table between the two chairs and weighed it in his hands. "Why didn't you ever have children, Natalie?"

I swallowed hard, "I wasn't able to."

"Is there something wrong with you?"

"Max, my husband…"

"He didn't want children?"

"No," I whispered.

"Anna told me that he was much older than you," Gunter said, still examining the marble ashtray. "Perhaps he couldn't have children."

"He wasn't able to…" I said looking down at the tablecloth to hide my humiliation.

"So Mila is like a daughter to you, yes?"

"Yes," I sighed.

"What will you do if her mother sends for her? What will you do then? You will have lost both your husband and your so-called 'daughter'."

I remained silent, what was there to say?

"You are still in love with him?"

"Yes."

"But he is gone. On the other hand, you are lucky. From what your sister says, you and Deszo have resumed the romance you began in college."

Deszo, wouldn't return my gaze.

Gunter continued, "Anna also said your husband was from Russia?"

"Yes," I replied.

"It's too bad he's not alive today. He could greet his fellow countrymen when they arrive. I wonder if they would be happy to see him. Or would they consider him a traitor?"

He put down the ashtray and went to the door of the suite. The young soldier who'd brought our meal stood at the door when Gunter opened it. They spoke to one another in low tones and then the soldier was gone.

Gunter closed the door, walked back to the chairs near the window, and sat down. He pulled an ornate silver cigarette case out of his jacket, opened it and then made an elaborate ritual out of selecting one. He then snapped the cover shut and tapped the cigarette on the edge of the case. He smiled and then flicked the cover open again.

"Excuse my manners. Deszo, would you join me over here for a smoke? Natalie, I think you'd be more comfortable if you remained at the table."

Deszo stood and walked across the room. He took one of the offered cigarettes and sat down in the chair next to Gunter.

The door to the suite opened and the young soldier appeared again. He supported Jozef under the arms and helped the beaten young boy into the room.

I rose from my seat to go to Jozef's side.

"Sit down."

"He's hurt. He needs help."

"If you don't sit down, I'll have him killed right now," Gunter said softly, as he stared at the boy and exhaled a grey stream of smoke.

Slowly, I returned to my seat not taking my eyes off Jozef. His head bobbed listlessly against his chest. His face was covered with blood, and the first bluish-purple swelling of bruises and fractured bone spread across his nose and cheeks. His eyes were swollen shut. His arms hung uselessly at his sides.

Gunter nodded toward Deszo's chair and the soldier slid it from the table to the center of the room and then dropped Jozef into the seat so that he sat like a border between me and Deszo and Gunter.

"Your first bargaining chip." Deszo took a drag of his cigarette and appraised the damage.

Gunter smiled and followed Deszo's gaze. He cocked his head to one side, "My men are sloppy."

"Natalie might feel some maternal instinct toward him," Deszo shrugged.

"But he's not your concern?"

Deszo sighed and watched Jozef struggle to sit upright in the chair and then fail as his legs slipped out from under him. A long, thin line of bloodied mucus ran from his nose to his chin and dangled toward his chest. "Anna and Mila are my concern."

"I understand that you are a frequent guest at the Swedish Consulate."

Deszo took a folded handkerchief from his pocket and tossed it toward Jozef's chair. The white square of cloth landed at Jozef's feet.

"I'd like to know if they are passing information on to the Allies, in addition to their manufacture of phony passports."

"Isn't that a rhetorical question?" Deszo asked.

Gunter tapped the ash of his cigarette into the ashtray and nodded. "Yes, but you know the substance of that information."

"You give me too much credit."

"I believe you are one of the suppliers."

"I've simply been trying to obtain passports for Natalie and Anna and Mila."

"That's not what your young friend says."

Our eyes traveled to Jozef as if waiting confirmation. He shook his head and mumbled something unintelligible through swollen, cracked lips.

"I've met the boy once," Deszo replied.

"He says that he's followed you."

"I'm not impressed," Deszo said. "He has no way of knowing my conversations."

"As he is no use to you or to us, he is a liability."

Gunter rose and walked over to Jozef. He stood behind Jozef's chair and pulled back his head by his hair, exposing his neck. The scar I'd seen on Gunter's neck flashed before my eyes. Jozef moaned but his words were lost in a gurgle of blood that dribbled from the corner of his mouth.

Gunter pulled a knife from his pocket and with a flick of his finger, exposed the long silvery blade.

"Deszo, stop him!" My voice was a hollow shriek in the stillness of the room. The two men stared at one another so entranced in their game that they took no notice of my presence. "Gunter, let him go, he's done nothing wrong. He knows nothing of Deszo's business."

"Perhaps you do."

I was shocked. Because of course I didn't. I'd known Deszo for over thirty years, and thought I knew him well. Even tonight, I'd imagined that Gunter was talking about a stranger as he described the meetings that Deszo was allegedly a party to. "I'm only trying to save my family."

"Natalie, leave the room," Deszo's voice was low and controlled. "Now. Go home."

"Let me take Jozef."

Gunter pressed the blade of the knife against Jozef's neck. I ran to his side and tried to grab his hand. He shoved me away and in the movement of his hand, a sliver of blood ran down Jozef's neck.

"Stop, please! Deszo, tell him what he wants to know."

"Gunter, lay down the knife and let's talk."

Gunter stared at Deszo and shook his head. "We now have three bodies to trade on."

"What do you want?"

"I want you to act as my emissary."

Deszo stood and moved toward Gunter. "Remove the knife from his neck and we'll talk."

Gunter pressed the knife tighter against Jozef's neck. The blood began to flow more freely. "Time is running out."

Deszo nodded and Gunter released Jozef from his grasp. I knelt at Jozef's side as he slid from the chair and onto the floor. I cradled him in my arms and used Deszo's handkerchief to stop the flow of blood. Gunter's dramatic act had only produced a surface wound but the blood soon soaked through the cloth, staining my fingers.

"I am meeting someone from the Swedish consulate in two days," Deszo said. "I will go to the meeting and then tell you what plans were discussed afterwards. You must release Anna and Mila before that or there will be no deal."

Gunter chuckled and wiped his hands with a napkin from the table. "Fair enough. You realize that if you don't deliver your end of the bargain, the consequences will be worse for everyone next time."

He tossed the napkin on the floor and walked toward the door. "You will find the girls at the ghetto, tomorrow morning. Shall we say, eight?"

We were left alone in the room. Deszo came to my side and helped me to lift Jozef. We carried him between us out of the room and through the now-empty living room.

On the sidewalk downstairs, the Nazi soldier who'd served our dinner stood holding open the back door of a car. "I will take you home." He took Jozef from us, put him into the back seat, and then walked around to the driver's side. We climbed in next to Jozef and I held him as we sped through the streets to my apartment.

Chapter Thirty

I put Jozef into Mila's bed and did my best to dress his wounds. Jozef grimaced in pain as I put a cold rag to his face. I began to unbutton his shirt and as I tried to slip the shirt over his shoulder, he cried out in pain. "I'll be right back," I said, returning with a pair of scissors.

"What are you doing?" he said.

"I have to cut your clothes off you."

"No!"

"I'll give you some of my husband's clothes to wear tomorrow." I moved his arm to his side and slowly cut the shirt away from his body. "In the meantime, this is the only way I can properly clean your wounds."

Once his upper body was exposed, I understood why he had cried out in pain. His shoulder was dislocated and his other arm appeared to be fractured at the wrist. In addition, his midsection was a mottled mass of blue green bruises.

As I unbuckled his belt and began to cut away his pants, Jozef turned his head in embarrassment. "You're not the first man I've seen," I said tenderly. I tried to maintain lightness in my voice, but it was difficult not to gag at the sight before me. Jozef's legs were dotted with open sores where cigarettes had burned holes through his skin. I wiped the beads of nervous sweat from my forehead. "My God, Jozef, how long did they torture you?"

He bit his lip and refused to answer.

"Jozef, did you hear them mention Mila and Anna while you were there? Do you know if they are still alive?"

He nodded his head. "I think so," he mumbled. "At least, Mila. They said she was sent to the ghetto. I heard someone say Anna's name, but I couldn't hear what they were saying, the others were laughing."

I cringed. Anna and Mila had been picked up

at different times. Anna first, and then Mila the following morning. It would have taken them some time to link them.

Had something Anna said caused them to watch the apartment and then follow Mila and Mrs. Szep when they left? But why didn't they pick them up immediately, why let them get to the house safely? And they'd only taken Mila, from what we'd heard, Mrs. Szep and her friend had been left unharmed.

I could only hope that Anna had been taken to the ghetto and managed to find Mila. But when she left, Mila was safely at home. Perhaps she still didn't know that Mila had been picked up. Or had Gunter told her?

I shivered at the thought. Then turned my attention back to Jozef's injuries, as I tried to apply ointment as gently as possible. Jozef had suffered so much, it would take him weeks to heal, but the psychological abuse he'd suffered would be with him much longer. "Mila would be proud of the way you've tried to help her. Thank you for your help, Jozef."

He shook his head, "I didn't mean for it to turn out this way."

"No one did," I said.

"There is a transport train leaving for the camps tomorrow," he whispered. He turned to look into my eyes. "Get to the ghetto earlier or you will miss them."

"But Deszo made a deal with Gunter."

He coughed and a sliver of blood seeped from the edge of his mouth. "He wants to dangle the bait in front of Deszo so that he'll go to the meeting. But he doesn't care whether they are safe or not."

~*~

Deszo and I sat side by side on the couch in my study. We'd pulled the shades on the window to conceal the weak light that emanated from two candle stubs that burned on the table in front of us. Deszo took my hand and pulled me to his side. I slipped easily under his arm and leaned my head against his shoulder. My arm rested against his chest, and we held each other with our eyes closed, breathing slowly until we exhaled and inhaled in tandem.

"Natalie, we will get through tomorrow together." Deszo turned in my embrace to face me. "I will not allow anything to happen to you."

I smiled gratefully. "Thank you for all you've done."

Deszo whispered, "I love you with all my heart. You know I always have."

"Please don't say that." I studied my hands and remembered my dream of Max. There was no going back for me. I couldn't pretend to feel something I didn't.

"Natalie, I know you still think of Max. I know you'll never love me that way. But in time…"

"Deszo, no," I sighed.

"After tomorrow, things will be better," he said, ignoring my words. "The war will be over soon. I'll make sure Anna is taken care of, and I'll do whatever you want about Mila. I'll help you find her mother, or I'll help you to raise her as our own."

"Deszo, stop! We've known each other since

we were children. You were Max's best friend. I love you as a friend, nothing more. And as for Anna and Mila..." A sob choked me. "I don't even know if Anna is still alive. Jozef says we have to get to the ghetto early tomorrow."

"Gunter wouldn't allow anything to happen to them."

I stopped, put my hand to my mouth, and then continued, "Deszo, which side do you work for?"

"Be careful what you ask, Natalie," he said, taking his hand out of mine.

"Are you already working with the Germans? Is that why Gunter singled you out?"

"Natalie, I can't discuss my role," he said. "There is too much at stake."

"For whom? For Anna, for Mila?"

"I am working for the good of our country."

"And the good of your family's business? Have the Germans promised to leave your father's business alone if you provide them with information?"

Suddenly I was dizzy and sick to my stomach. "Did you have anything to do with Anna's capture? Do you know where they have taken her?"

"I don't know where Anna is," Deszo said.

My heart turned cold. I didn't know what to believe anymore. Clearly, I needed Deszo in order to get Mila and Anna back. But beyond that, I didn't believe I could trust him. I got up and moved to a chair across the room.

Deszo was clearly exasperated. "Natalie, have you considered Anna's possible part in Mila's capture?"

"When she left the apartment, the plan to send Mila away hadn't been created."

"But she knew that Mila was being hidden."

"Why would she do something to harm Mila? She's her aunt."

"Yes, but you're the one who has the real connection to Mila. And Anna was furious with you, because in her delusional mind we were starting an affair."

"Anna is sick, not sadistic." My knuckles were white underneath my grip on the arms of the chair. "And you knew where Mila was being taken. Anna didn't."

"Natalie, I have no motivation to harm Mila. Anna does."

I thought for a minute.

"Deszo, there's something I have been meaning to ask you. If you do have connections that can help get Mila to a safe house, then why didn't you try and help her sooner? You knew she was Jewish and did nothing until, out of desperation, I begged you to help us. Remember? On that awful day with Anna at the university? Why didn't you think of offering your help to us before then? "

Deszo seemed to want to defend himself, but hesitated and remained silent. "There were things that I didn't want to reveal at that time. There are so many lives at stake, more than just one or two."

His eyes revealed shame and failure. He turned from me and looked at the floor. I could feel his sense of being trapped in his circumstances, but weren't we all? Although no one is ever really certain what the right thing to do is in times of crisis, I knew that if Max were in the same position he would have done things differently. Max was the better man. I knew it all along.

Chapter Thirty-One

The small clock on the bookshelf chimed five times. We'd fallen asleep on opposite sides of the room. I got up and shook Deszo's arm gently and whispered, "It's time."

At the front door, we put on our coats and made our way down the stairs and into the still dark, pre-dawn streets.

The hired car that Deszo had arranged was waiting at the curb. The driver acknowledged us with a curt nod as we bundled into the back seat. The car leapt and raced along side streets until we reached the first building on the street designated as the Jewish ghetto.

As the car pulled to a stop, we jumped out and ran to the heavy metal gates that now stood open and unguarded. We stopped in our tracks at the sight of the empty buildings.

"It's too late!" My knees buckled. "They've taken them to the train station."

"Let's go." Deszo wrapped a protective arm around me and guided me back to the waiting car. I sank into the leather back seat as the car lurched. Deszo held my hand, and I prayed that we wouldn't be too late.

The train station was a horror. As Deszo showed our papers to a man guarding the entrance, I looked hopelessly at the swarm of people.

Soldiers lined the platform; they were herding throngs of bewildered Jews into cattle cars. Their luggage was left in heaps, promised to be on the next train, though I doubt anyone believed this lie anymore.

Why were they allowing themselves to be shoved onto trains that were certainly taking them to their death? My anger flared, why didn't anyone turn and resist? The number of captives far outnumbered their guards.

"They outnumber the Nazis, why don't they turn and fight?" I hissed under my breath.

Deszo motioned toward the machine gun that was held by one solider, as another Nazi used a bayonet to prod an elderly man who wasn't moving fast enough. "It would be a massacre. The Nazis don't care if they kill them here or at the camps. But each one getting on the train hopes they will be the one who survives."

As I yelled for Anna and Mila, Deszo pushed a path ahead of us. The soldiers laughed at my useless efforts and suggested that we could easily join the passengers on the train if we'd like a closer look.

Deszo grabbed one of the men, demanded to be shown the officer in charge, and was pointed to a lone figure further down the platform.

I followed their gaze and then gasped when I saw Gunter staring at us, smiling as he checked his watch.

"You're early," he said.

"You lied to us! You never meant to set them free."

Gunter shrugged. "There's nothing I can do."

"You'll find them now, or there will be no

meeting," Deszo said.

The two men stared at each other, and it seemed that Deszo had whispered a name or a phrase under his breath, which I couldn't hear, but had the effect of causing Gunter's eye to twitch imperceptibly. Finally, when some internal scale tipped in our favor, Gunter relented.

He called over two young soldiers each holding a clipboard filled with lists of names. He took the clipboards and flipped through the pages.

Gunter barked an order and two soldiers jumped into action running from train to train screaming the names of Mila and Anna.

Each closed door of the loaded cars was opened, revealing a scene from hell. People were crushed together, with no room to move. They stretched out their arms as the door opened and pleaded to be set free. A soldier holding a gun pointed at them was the only thing that kept the occupants from tumbling out.

Door after door opened and closed. One, two, three, five, six…where were they?

Another door opened, and from the back, I

heard Mila's voice above the others.

"Yes! Yes, it's Mila!"

The soldier screamed for the occupants of the car to move aside to let Mila come to the front.

Mila tumbled onto the platform, and I ran and swept her into my embrace. "You're safe now."

Behind us, the soldier closed the door to the train car.

"But where's Anna? Mila, was Anna in the car with you?"

Mila shook her head. "I don't know where Anna is. I never saw her."

"Deszo, help me! We've got to find Anna!"

We ran to the nearest open car and yelled for Anna. We went down the row to each car, calling her name. There was no answer. Behind us, each door closed.

We reached the final car, still no answer to our calls for Anna. I turned to the soldier standing next to me, "We must keep trying. Ask them to open the doors again."

The young soldier turned to me and then to Gunter.

"Don't you understand?" I pleaded. "She's my sister. She doesn't belong on that train."

The young soldier shrugged. "Everyone in the ghetto is there for a reason."

"It was your doing!" I grabbed the lapels of Gunter's coat. "Make them search the trains again."

He firmly pried my fingers from his coat held them at my sides to create a distance between our bodies. "We have a schedule to keep."

"No, please. Please you must give me one more chance to find her!"

The train's whistle blew, and Deszo yelled for me, "Natalie!"

"I have to find her, help me, Deszo."

He ran over to Gunter. Deszo pulled a handful of money out of his coat pocket. Gunter pushed the money away, shook his head and gestured toward the train. I couldn't hear their voices, but the message was clear.

"Put me on the train!"

"Natalie, no!" Deszo said.

Gunter studied my face. "Where these trains are going, there is no return. This is not a game."

"I don't care."

"Natalie." Deszo grabbed my arm and pulled me to his side. "You can't help her now."

"I can. I must."

"It's too late," Deszo said. "Look."

The train was beginning to move.

"Get me on the train!" I screamed.

"We'll send a message up the line and if she's on the train, tell them to take her out of the line at the camp," Gunter said.

"NO! I must go with her!"

"How can you get on this train, knowing where it is going?"

"She is my sister."

Gunter shouted to one of the soldiers, who in turn, blew a whistle and the train halted. The soldiers went to the nearest train car and slid open the door.

"Deszo, take care of Mila. Use your contacts to get her to the United States. Max has cousins there in New York, and she can stay with them. That's the only place she will be safe. Make sure she gets through this. Will you?"

Deszo bit his lip, reluctantly nodding his assent.

"Please don't leave me, Nana." Mila grabbed my sleeve and wept.

I touched her cheek and quickly kissed her. "I must do this, my sweetheart. You will be safe now, I promise. But who will care for Anna if I don't go? She needs me now. You understand, don't you?"

"Let someone else take care of Anna, you have to stay here and take care of me!"

"Mila," I crooned caressing her tear-stained cheeks. "I have always loved you as if you were my own daughter. I will always love you, no matter what happens. Go with Deszo and let him send you out of this country, where you will be safe. I promise to join you as soon as I can."

"You can't leave me alone!"

"God will be with you."

"No, He won't. Where is He now?"

I pressed my lips together in a tight-lipped smile and my eyes moved from her face to the train behind me. "He is there, on that train, with His children. God's love will never leave you, Mila.

And now I must go to be with my sister. Anna won't know what to do without me."

Deszo shook his head as he eased Mila from my embrace and held her protectively against his side. "Natalie, stay here and let me see what I can do to help Anna from this end."

"I can't. She won't survive long enough without my protection. We will rely on you to help us from here, while I do my best to protect her."

"What if you don't find her, or what if her mind is so far gone that she doesn't even recognize you?"

"She is still my sister, and I can't knowingly turn my back on her if there is still hope." My smile was feeble, but strong. "You take care of Mila, and I will see you both soon."

I walked to the door of the train and a man held out his hand to help me up. I turned to thank him and found myself staring into the eyes of my beloved, Max.

Behind us, the door slid shut, plunging us into darkness.

Epilogue

Mila Goes Home

Mrs. Tuesday walked down the long row of graves. In the far corner, she found the one she was looking for. She laid a new row of dried breadcrumbs along the top of the stone marker and stood for a moment breathing in the cold air.

"Hello Uncle Max," she said. "It's good to be home."

There was no reply to her greeting. She understood that she did not have the special communion with the dead that her Aunt Natalie had possessed. But she continued to speak aloud, because it was easier, and because she needed to hear her own words.

"I've been to our old apartment. Can you imagine? They've divided it into three little apartments now.

There are shops on the ground floor. One's a bakery that makes the nut rolls you adored. They're not as good as Mrs. Szep's but they taste better than anything that I could get in the States.

"The letter I received explained everything that happened after I was sent away from Budapest.

"First, I want to thank you and thank God for the kindness of your family. Your cousins took me in when I got off the boat, alone, with one satchel of clothing, and a letter. They gave me a home and raised me as if I was your daughter. Thanks to their generosity, I went to university and created a successful life for myself in New York.

"I like to think that your spirit was with me during those first lonely years, in that new country. Just as you were with your beloved, Natalie through her darkest days.

Unfortunately, my other allies were not so lucky after that fateful day on the train platform, although we all tried our best to begin new lives. Jozef survived the torture of the Nazi's. Deszo worked to get him on the same boat as me to the United States.

"On the day we were supposed to leave, Jozef

refused to join me. He said he had a new 'business opportunity' to take care of his family. The Communists killed him two years later. Deszo met the same fate, although he should have been hailed as a national hero for his resistance of first the Nazis, and then the Communists.

"And Nana got on the train. First, we tried to stop her. Then, after she was gone, we tried to find her, to tell the Nazis that there had been a terrible mistake and that she should not have been taken to the camps. But, of course, our story sounded like every other. No one would listen to us. And Natalie was swallowed up in the monster.

"Do you remember the favorite verse of Anna and Natalie? 'Now faith is the substance of things hoped for, the evidence of things not seen.' We all believed that faith was our basis in hope.

"We didn't understand that the verse pertained to faith in God. Not in each other. I am as guilty as the rest. How many years have I hoped for my mother's love? For how many years after that day at the train station did I hate God even more than the Nazis for taking away

Natalie, who loved me as my mother should have?

"Nana got on the train." Mrs. Tuesday carefully lowered herself onto a bench near the grave. She gently rocked back and forth, rubbing her hands over her arms to warm herself.

Eventually, she unfolded the letter she'd carried in her coat pocket since leaving New York. She put on her reading glasses and read, for the tenth or twentieth time, the pages that had been folded into that overstuffed envelope.

"This report was made by talking to eyewitnesses who were there. Not really them, but their children. Bits of information were pieced together from records that were found later.

"Nana got off the train when it reached the camps. She searched for Anna, but when she found her it was too late. As Deszo predicted, Anna's mind had escaped the horror that surrounded her.

"They say in this letter that Anna was always on

her way to the opera. That she sat staring at a wall that she claimed to be a mirror where she'd gently rub her face with dirt and claim it was makeup. Despite the horrific deprivation, the accounts say she was cheerful. In her few lucid moments, Anna would recite poetry for the other women to encourage them.

"They write that Natalie spent many hours talking out loud to God. Literally talking to Him as if He was right there with them in the camps. When she wasn't talking to God, she was talking to someone named 'Max'. We know who that was, don't we?

"Deszo tried to save them. Before he put me on the ship for the States, I saw him go out countless evenings to meet with Nazi officers that swore they had contacts at the camps who could find Natalie and Anna and free them. I think in the end, Deszo realized it was a fool's errand, and his bribes were going nowhere.

"I hate to think of Natalie wondering where we were or when help would arrive. I know she did her best to take care of Anna. She explained to anyone who would listen that there had been a mistake, they were not meant

to be there. But then again, no one was meant to be there, were they?

"The Nazi's were very interested in them when they realized they were twins, that one had gone insane while the other remained intact. They wanted to use them in medical experiments.

"But you see they ran out of time. The Allies were coming. So they did what all bad children do, they tried to hide their sins, to clean up the mess before they were caught. Some were lucky; they were sent to other camps and survived.

"Some years later, Natalie's diaries were discovered after her apartment had been deemed abandoned and her belongings looted. They didn't quite know what to do with her journals, so they sold them with the rest of her books at a local bookshop. Luckily, someone recognized her work as a children's author and then discovered her private papers among the manuscripts. They also discovered the story she wrote as she imagined my future.

"As a tribute to her death, the Hungarian State Publishing Cooperative published a heavily edited

version of her diaries along with her story about Mrs. Tuesday. I'm told that for years they even tried to find me, luckily without success.

"Now, all these years later, after the fall of the Soviet Union, and the ease of finding someone with computers, the journals and Mrs. Tuesday's story found their way to me."

Mila patted the top of the gravestone. "And now I have finally come home."

She bowed her head, closed her eyes, and folded her hands in her lap. She recalled all the pain she'd carried for the many years after that fateful day, how she swore God could not exist if He'd let such horror go unchecked.

After the package arrived, she'd begun to read Natalie's journals, of her love for Jesus, of His willingness to die to save others. Mila began to understand that her aunt was able to get on that train with the knowledge that no matter what happened, God would be with her.

Reading those journals had been Mila's path back to church, and eventually back to God. Yes, there had been many nights of tears. Nights of anguished prayers that threatened to break her heart open again with the pain of the unearthed memories. Yet, eventually Mila's heart opened to the saving grace God offered and the peace that came for the first time in her life.

"Max, they say that when Nana and Anna were sent to the gas chambers, they were holding hands and smiling. They say that Nana was talking to God. Were you with her, as well?"

Mrs. Tuesday clasped her hands together, and carefully placed them in her lap.

"And what about you dear God?" she asked titling her head back to look at the steel grey sky. "Were You with them in their darkest hour? I like to imagine You were with each of us from the very beginning."

'Now faith is the substance of things hoped for, the evidence of things not seen.'

THE END

From The Author

If you enjoyed *Mrs. Tuesday's Departure*, would you please take a moment to leave a review on Amazon.com or Goodreads.com, or your favorite book site?

Sharing your enjoyment of a book helps to spread the word and is more important to an author than anything else!

Please keep reading for the first chapter from my novel *God Loves You. –Chester Blue*, as well as an excerpt from *Trusting God with Your Dream*.

You can also visit my website to sign-up for news about upcoming books and giveaways: www.suzanneelizabethanderson.com

God Bless You!

BOOKS BY

SUZANNE ELIZABETH ANDERSON

Mrs. Tuesday's Departure

God Loves You. ~ Chester Blue

Trusting God with Your Dream: A 31-Day Devotional for Young Women

The Night of the Great Polar Bear

God Loves Your Dream: A 60-Day Devotional

Journey Toward God's Dream for You

Love in a Time of War

A Map of Heaven

Henry's Guide to Happiness

God Loves You.
—Chester Blue

By Suzanne Elizabeth Anderson

Chapter One

"My Goodness, there are so many stars out tonight," Miss Millie whispered. She stood on her back porch; hands on her hips, head tilted back, and stared at the glittering night sky.

Finally, she found her favorite constellation, the Big Dipper. "How lucky we are to have such wondrous stars to enjoy."

Each night she came outside to admire the moon and the blanket of twinkling stars that covered the sky from one end to the other. She'd been doing this for most of her seventy-five years on Earth.

Some nights, the stars formed the shapes of animals romping through the sky, like the Big

Dipper, which formed part of the Ursa Major, called that because 'ursa' meant 'bear' and it resembled a big bear in the sky. Which is exactly why it was her favorite. Miss Millie had a very special place in her heart for bears.

For Miss Millie, each night held a new adventure as she watched the stars move across the sky with the changing seasons. And each night she made a wish on the first star she saw. Most nights, Miss Millie's heart was filled with joy at the beauty of the night sky. But tonight was so very different. It was the end of a long day that had brought terrible news. Instead of smiling as she stared at the panorama overhead, she pursed her lips to keep from crying and her eyes filled with tears and blurred the stars she loved so dearly.

Tonight she had a special wish. She walked down the steps of the porch and out to the backyard. The grass was wet and cool beneath her bare feet. Miss Millie looked up at the sky and thought about the right way to phrase her wish. She needed to think carefully, because this wasn't an ordinary wish. It was going to be a prayer. And prayers were more powerful than wishes.

Lately she'd been bothered that the world had forgotten the magic of wishes and dreams. Nowadays, it seemed that people looked down instead of up. They went to work, they came home, and then they went to sleep. It seemed that most people moved through their lives as if they were sleepwalking.

Miss Millie understood how this could easily happen. Some people gave up on their wishes and dreams because they'd been disappointed too many times in life and just didn't have the courage to keep hoping things would change.

That's what had happened in the little Midwestern town where Miss Millie had lived her whole life. It had been a gradual thing, but like rust, some gradual things can be deadly. When she was a little girl, her hometown of Blossom, Ohio, was a vibrant place, full of young families. No matter how many books about faraway places young Millie read, she couldn't imagine living anywhere else.

Which is why, when Miss Millie grew up, she

opened a shop on Main Street. Main Street was always filled with beautiful shops and shoppers so it was the perfect place to open a store.

In her shop, Miss Millie sold and repaired all sorts of teddy bears. With all those young families, Miss Millie's shop was always busy. Young children came with their parents to choose their first bear. Adults came to have their cherished childhood bears fixed after they'd been loved through many years and needed a stitch to repair a tear, or new eyes or ears. Her shop even attracted teddy bear collectors, who knew that Miss Millie had a secret supply of very old, very special bears that she could sometimes be convinced to sell to a special home.

As the years, and then decades flew by, Miss Millie became known as the best teddy bear historian and repairwoman in the Midwest. Some people said she was even the best in the entire United States.

But then the children of the young families became adults and went off to college. And never returned home to Blossom to start their own families. At first no one noticed that the shops on Main Street were quieter than usual, or that the Main Street Diner never filled up after the morning rush of farmers who stopped by for breakfast at five a.m.

Even Miss Millie didn't notice at first. She still received a lot of business through the mail, for bears that needed to be repaired, or requests for a search for a rare bear that a collector was hoping to find. But then one day Miss Mille looked up from her table at the back of the shop where she usually spent her day working, and noticed that she was alone.

The next day it was the same. And the day after that. So she went to see her friend, Lulu, the waitress at the Main Street Diner and asked her if she'd also noticed fewer people on Main Street.

"Fewer people, on Main Street?" Lulu threw back her head and laughed. She laughed so hard, she had to put down the pot of coffee she'd holding to pour Miss Millie's second cup. "Honey, it's not just Main Street, this whole town is as quiet as a church on Monday. So many people have moved away, I believe we're the town that's been forgotten."

Miss Millie looked down at her cup of coffee and frowned. This was terrible news. Blossom was a wonderful town. Yes, it was a small town and perhaps not as exciting as a big city. But there were so many good things about it. Why had people given up and moved away?

That was a month ago. Since that conversation with Lulu, things had gotten worse. Once Miss Millie had started to pay attention, she realized that at times a whole week would go by without a single person coming into her shop. And on her walk home at the end of the day, she began to notice that more and more of the stores that shared Main Street were closing or were already empty.

And then today, Miss Millie had received the worst news of all. Mr. Jones, the man who owned the building, which housed her teddy bear shop, had lost the building to the bank. The bank was going to sell the building at auction, which meant that Miss Millie could no longer have a teddy bear shop in his building. She would have to move.

This was of course terrible news. Not only would Miss Millie lose her shop, she would lose her business. Yes, yes, perhaps she could open a new shop in one of the many other empty stores on Main Street. But this was the proof that it wouldn't matter where she moved, there were simply not enough people in Blossom to shop in her teddy bear store.

Which is why tonight she stood staring up at the stars with a special purpose in her heart. Miss Millie believed in dreams and wishes. And tonight she was going to pray for some way to share her belief with others.

"Dear God," Miss Millie began as she looked up at the stars, "how many people never see how beautiful the sky is at night because they simply don't take the time to look up?"

She smiled as a shooting star flew through the dark sky.

"Maybe it's because we seem to be going through a tough time right now. I suppose when times are tough people don't have time for teddy bears or small towns like Blossom. I know that You are the Creator of all things. And I know, when things look the worst is when something new and wonderful is about to happen, if we can just hold on. Now that my teddy bear shop is closed I don't know what I'm going to do. I don't know what's going to happen to my hometown, but You do." Miss Millie said. "Dear God, I'm holding on, but I could sure use a bit of help from You. Give me a way to share the gift of believing in dreams with others, too."

Miss Millie stretched out her arms and embraced all the beauty she saw in the sky above her head. She silently thanked God for creating such a beautiful universe where anything was possible even when it seemed impossible.

She smiled as she saw another star shooting across the sky. "Thank you, God." And she turned and went back in the house to go to bed.

The next morning, Miss Millie woke up early. She climbed from her bed and stretched her arms over her head and then twisted from side to side to get her creaky old bones and muscles warmed up to start the day.

As she turned, she glanced out of her bedroom window, and saw that it was a glorious, sunny, summer morning.

She threw on her robe and hurried downstairs; she needed to make her breakfast and get to the shop. On such a beautiful morning there were certain to be lots of people on Main Street and that meant there might be some new customers for her shop!

Then she stopped on the bottom step and touched her fingertips to her lips as she remembered that her shop was closing. There wouldn't be lots of people on Main Street. So many of the stores were empty, no one came to Main Street anymore. If they needed anything, they went to the big mall, in the big town, down the hill.

Suddenly she felt very sad about closing her store and facing the future alone. What would she do? Miss Millie blinked back the tears. No, she thought, I won't cry, I know that when things are at their worst, something better is just around the corner if we just put one foot in front of the other and keep moving. She grasped the banister railing tightly and straightened her back with her new resolve. Her heart still hurt, and she was more than a little bit afraid of not knowing what to do next, but she would take her own advice.

Well then, this morning would be the perfect time to work in her garden! She needed to weed the flowerbed and then she would tie up the beans in the vegetable garden. If she was lucky, the cabbage and zucchini would be ready to harvest and she would be able to make soup for tonight's dinner.

Later, she would go to her shop on Main Street and begin packing her teddy bears. She would make a list of all the people she knew who might want to buy one of the remaining bears, then she'd pick a few that she could donate to the children's hospital, and finally, she would bring the rest home. They would sit on the shelves of her office until she figured out what to do next.

First though, she would pick up the newspaper from the front porch, make coffee, have a bite to eat, put on her overalls and her green rubber clogs, and then she'd be ready to work in the garden.

She'd finished making her mental list of things to do, just as she opened the front door to pick up her morning newspaper.

Right next to her newspaper, she found a box wrapped in plain brown paper and tied with twine. Miss Millie's name and address was printed in big red letters in the lower right corner. As she looked closer, she noticed there was no return address to be found anywhere. Who had sent the box?

Miss Millie picked up the box and her newspaper and brought them both into the kitchen where she placed them on the table while she made a pot of coffee and a piece of toast for her breakfast. She carefully cut the piece of toast in half. On one half she spread a spoonful of peanut butter and on the other half she spread a spoonful of chocolate hazelnut spread. This was her favorite breakfast for sunny days. She sat down at the table with her cup of coffee and her plate of toast and carefully considered the box as she ate her breakfast.

She hadn't ordered anything, so that couldn't be it.

She chewed her toast and thought very

carefully.

It wasn't her birthday.

She took a sip of coffee, and thought more deeply.

It was the end of August. Schools had just started, perhaps it was a box of notebooks and pencils that were meant for a young student who lived nearby?

Miss Millie checked the address again. No, it was her name and address clearly printed on the front of the box.

Christmas was still four months away.

Perhaps, it was time to stop staring at the box and take action.

Miss Millie moved her cup and plate to the side of the table and placed the box in front of her. Very carefully, she cut the twine and unwrapped the brown paper that covered the box. Beneath the plain brown paper was a cardboard box with a lid. It was a plain orange box with no writing anywhere that might give a hint as to what was inside. So Miss Millie lifted the lid of the box.

And was very surprised by what she saw.

Trusting God with Your Dream

By Suzanne Elizabeth Anderson

Introduction

One Christmas, my mother gave me a copy of The Daily Walk Bible. I'd tried daily reading-plan Bibles before without the dedication to make it beyond a cursory reading that ended sometime in January. But this time was different.

What kept me motivated (especially as I slogged through those difficult Old Testament books) was that I'd reached a crossroads in my life and I was seeking life-changing responses to my unanswered prayers about career and finances.

God had gone silent when I needed Him most and I was trying to find out why. Although I believed I'd prayed in good faith, and prayed "without ceasing", it seemed that nothing I did brought an answer to my prayers. It wasn't that

God wasn't there; He just wasn't listening to me.

After a year in the Bible, I came to a startling realization. All this time that I was waiting on God for an answer, I wasn't waiting alone. God was with me.

God used my year of waiting not to frustrate me, or abandon me, but to draw me into a closer relationship with Him.

As you read through these 31 days of devotionals, I pray that you too will be drawn closer to God.

In these pages, you will discover:

God will always provide an answer to your prayer.

You are never alone. God is always near.

And more than anything else…

God loves you beyond measure.

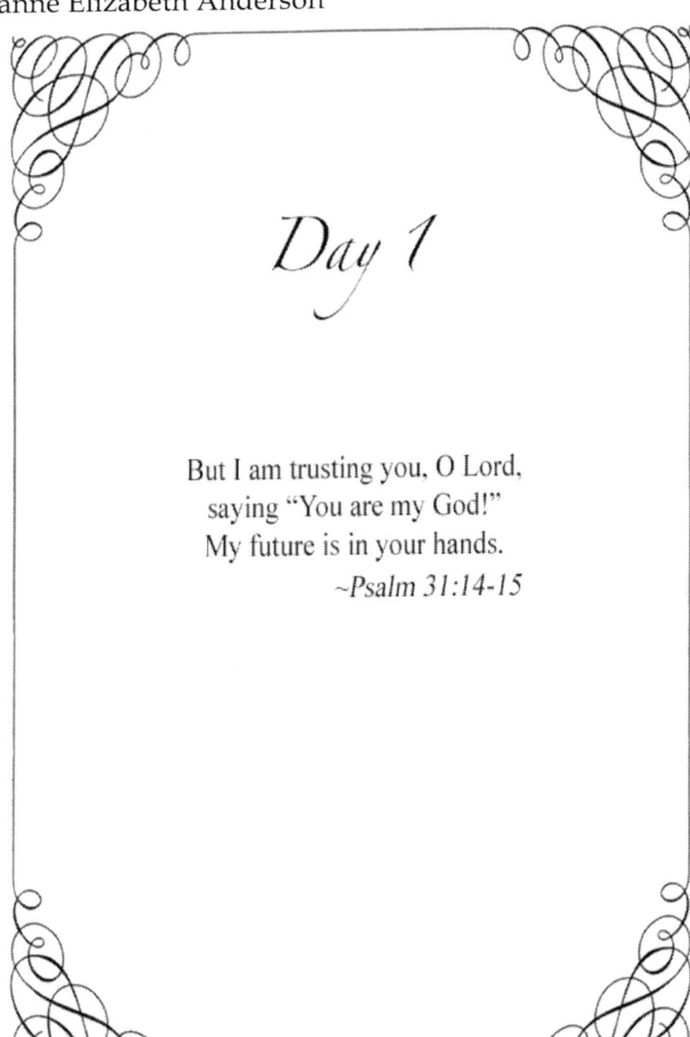

Day 1

But I am trusting you, O Lord,
saying "You are my God!"
My future is in your hands.
~Psalm 31:14-15

Day 1

Trusting God With Your Future

Talk about a dive into the deep end. What a great way to start our devotional journey!

Do we trust God enough to not only say: "You are my God, my future is in your hands!"

But to believe it and live it?

If you're not quite ready to make this commitment to God today, let's make it our goal to be there at the end of 31 days together.

If you're like me and have tried to do everything on your own, the most difficult decision may be letting go and letting God. What an enormous amount of trust it takes to say, "Okay God, I've tried to do it my way, but I'm ready to let go of the reins and turn my life over to you."

My first reaction to that announcement has

always been: But what if I don't like the plans God has for my life?

Don't worry. We're going to tackle that question within these pages.

This conflict of asking for God's help but not totally trusting His ability or willingness to answer, was what finally made me turn to the Bible in search of guidance and to many, many hours of prayer to seek God. In the end, I was able to say, "God you're in charge of my business, my finances, my life".

In the past, I tried to do it all myself. With mixed results.

Now, I declare that I am asking for God's blessing on my future and trust in Him to work it out for the best.

Will you join me to trust God with your present and your future?

mrs. tuesday's departure

Printed in Great Britain
by Amazon

35440635R00218